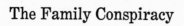

The Family Conspiracy

by the same author
THE BOUNDARY RIDERS

The Family Conspiracy

JOAN PHIPSON

Illustrated by Margaret Horder

Harcourt, Brace & World, Inc., New York

Contents

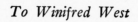

To Winifred West

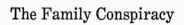

The Family Conspiracy

1: Mrs. Barker Frightens Her Family

It was in the middle of the night that Lorna first realized something was wrong. It seemed to her she had been asleep for hours when she awoke in a rather dazed, heavy way and gradually felt that everything was not as it should be. She lay quietly for a while, letting the ordinary daytime thoughts feel their way back into her brain. Little by little they ousted the sleepy half dreams that still clung about like cobwebs, and she knew at last she had been hearing noises that should not be going on at such an hour of the night. She opened her eyes and could just make out, between her own bed and the open window, the outline of her sister Belinda's body. At any rate, it was not Belinda who had awakened her. Then she saw something out of the corner of her eye and turned her head. Under the door came a little moving beam of light, as if someone had gone quietly past with a flashlight.

Now she could make out the muffled sounds of movement, and she thought she could catch the low murmur of voices. They sounded, as far as she could tell, like familiar voices, but in their soft tone she thought she could detect an urgency that made her heart beat a little more quickly than usual.

The only thing she could be certain of was that whatever it was that had awakened some of the family, it could not have anything to do with her, or they would have awakened her, too. She had just made up her mind that the sensible thing would be for her to turn over and try to go to sleep again when the telephone rang. The one long, shrill summons that meant that someone in the house was trying to rouse the Bungaree operator sounded outrageously loud in the quiet night. It made her jump so that the bed creaked.

Her nerves had just ceased to tingle when it rang again, and she remembered that it would probably have to ring several times before they succeeded in waking the boy who was supposed to be on duty all night at the exchange. It was always an even chance whether he could be persuaded to answer or not. Four times it rang, and each succeeding time the person at the telephone twirled the handle longer and more furiously. There was no question now of not trying to wake the rest of the family. Lorna was sure that none of them could have slept through such a performance; yet the long, regular breathing from Belinda's bed did not waver, and there was no movement from Fanny's little cot.

At last she heard her father's voice, with a sharper edge in it than usual, say, "You awake? Sure? Then get me

Doctor Roberts' house as quickly as you can, please."
There was a pause then, but Lorna did not wait for any
more. She knew she could not be wanted; she knew that she
should stay patiently where she was until someone came
and told her what was the matter. But almost before she
realized what was happening, her legs had poked themselves out from under the blankets. She threw back the
sheet and slid out. She was wide awake now and shivering
a little after the warmth of the bed. Her throat felt as if
there were a tight band around it, and she could not swallow properly. She went cautiously toward the door,
opened it, and crept out, shutting it soundlessly behind her.
There was a light coming from her mother's room and
another from the kitchen. The telephone was in the front
hall, beyond the bedroom, and she knew that her father
must still be standing there. She made her way to the
kitchen, expecting to find her mother there.

But her mother was not in the kitchen—only Jack, poking sticks into the grate of the stove in a feverish kind of
way while blue smoke poured out from every crack and
crevice. The kettle sat hopefully above the crackling sticks.
Lorna went quickly up to him.

"You've got the damper shut," she said and, leaning over,
pulled out the little iron bar that allowed the smoke to escape up the chimney. The last little wisp of smoke vanished.

"Oh heck," said Jack, looking up. "I'm in such a hurry
to get this darned kettle to boil I'm not thinking what I'm
doing." He looked around suddenly and saw that it was
Lorna who stood behind him.

"Hello," he said in surprise. "You were supposed not to
be awakened. Oh well—" He turned back to the stove.

The muscles of his face were drawn tight, and he looked tired.

Lorna had a feeling that he was going to forget her if she did not speak, so she said, "Jack, what's the matter? Why is Dad ringing up Doctor Roberts?"

"It's Mum," said Jack shortly. "She's sick."

Lorna felt her stomach muscles lurch. "Is she—is she very sick, Jack?" she asked, and her voice wobbled in the middle.

Jack looked up quickly then, and his face relaxed and softened. Squatting by the stove, with Lorna standing beside him, he put an arm around her quickly. He was not usually demonstrative, and she felt surprised and comforted.

"We don't know yet," he said in a more human voice than he had yet used. "Dad said she woke up feeling very bad, but she's a bit better now, and we thought a drink of tea might make her feel even better. If only I could get this"—he took a breath—"stove to go. I light the thing every morning, so you'd think I could do it now." He rammed in another piece of wood as he spoke.

"I'll do it," said Lorna, giving him a little push. "You're not really thinking, are you? You go and help Dad."

He got up quickly. At that moment they could hear Mr. Barker start to talk on the telephone.

"I'll be back in a tick," said Jack and made for the door.

Lorna bent down and started to coax the fire into more active life. Then she half emptied the kettle—so that it would boil more quickly—into a saucepan, for no member of the Barker family was ever guilty of throwing good water away. She could not quite hear what was going on on the telephone, and somehow she was glad that she could not. She concentrated on her job of getting the kettle to boil and found that it soothed her.

The kettle was just beginning to sing when she heard the little tinkle of the telephone being rung off, and Jack came back to the kitchen with his father. "Good for you," he said when he saw it. "I'll take a cup to Mum, and then I think we'll all have one."

Mr. Barker, a wild, disheveled figure in his pajamas, sprang up from the chair he had absentmindedly sat down on. "Give it to me," he said. "I'll take it." He almost snatched the cup from Jack and hurried to the door with it, spilling some into the saucer as he went.

"Dad's a bit cut up," Jack said, feeling that his father's impetuousness needed some explanation. "He can't stand seeing Mum sick."

"Is the doctor coming?" asked Lorna.

Jack nodded. "Said he'd come right away. He's a good sort."

They poured themselves cups of tea and pulled chairs up to the warmth of the stove. It was a warm summer night, but the fire in the stove was comforting.

"The other kids didn't wake up?" asked Jack, looking around, half expecting the ubiquitous Fanny to be lurking under the table.

"No," said Lorna. "No one but me, and I couldn't help coming when I heard Dad asking for the doctor."

"We didn't want to wake you," said Jack. "But you can't use that phone at night without waking the dead. You could go to bed again now if you like."

"Could I possibly stay till the doctor comes?" asked Lorna. "I couldn't sleep now, anyway."

"Suppose you can," said Jack. "Mum would send you

back, you know. But it would be a pity to risk waking the others."

So Lorna sat with Jack in the kitchen and waited for the doctor. Mr. Barker did not appear again, but they could hear the low murmur of voices coming from their mother's room. Why it should be more reassuring than silence they did not know, but it was.

The Barkers lived in the western part of New South Wales—not, however, in that challenging country known as the Far West, where the flat Australian plains stretch for miles and the violent seasons provide either a feast or a famine but never a compromise of bread and butter without jam. They lived rather in the Central West, just before the turbulent hills give place to the more tranquil, rolling, but hotter country beyond. Mr. Barker's father had taken up the property in the days when land was cheap and plentiful if one went far enough from civilization, and this had seemed quite far enough to him. Unfortunately, he had not been a sufficiently shrewd judge of country to pick one of the richer pieces of ground, and by the time he discovered his mistake, civilization had stretched a little farther and prices had risen. So the Barkers stayed where they were and did the best they could.

They ran sheep over the whole of the property, grew oats on the few flat acres there were to supplement the feed in winter, and maintained a constant war on the rabbits, which, in that honeycombed limestone country, threatened from time to time to overwhelm them. A river twisted its way among the hills and provided an occasional trout, numbers of water rats, and once, so Mr. Barker had said, a platypus. But that was in the days when it was almost virgin bush. The Barker children would not have parted with their river for all the new and stately homesteads of New South Wales.

They lived in the long, low weatherboard house that Mr. Barker's father had put up, and they played in the tangled wreck of the ambitious garden he had planted. The pepper trees that he put in were now gnarled and old, the shrubs had long since developed a vast middle-aged spread, and the roses rambled at will, threatening to smother them in a Sleeping Beauty embrace. But it was more than their home; it was their world, and until they became old enough to go to boarding school, as Lorna and Edward now were, they knew no other. Nor did they wish to, for they led full and busy lives.

Only Mr. and Mrs. Barker noticed that sometimes their life was rather too full. For Mr. Barker, though, the worst was over. Until recently he had had only one man to help him, and with the rabbiting, milking, and killing of cattle for meat as constant jobs, this was little enough. Now he had Jack, his eldest son, who had recently left school, and he felt that at last he could see daylight ahead.

But for Mrs. Barker there was as yet no end in sight. With a family of six, the cooking, housework, and washing alone could occupy all of every day, for she had no help and expected none. But until the children were old enough to go to boarding school, she conducted their correspondence school as well. And only a few days before she had cheerfully helped the children to organize a barbecue party for as many of their friends as they could manage to feed, and though her family rallied around, it was, as usual, Mrs. Barker who saw that things ran smoothly and who bore the brunt of the extra work. It was no wonder that she was thin and already gray and had a tired shadow under her

eyes that never left them. But there was a sharp, birdlike
alertness about her, too, and some of the lines around her
eyes were lines of laughter. Her family adored her, relied
on her, and worked her to the bone, and she was thankful
that she did not have her work to do, as many women
farther west had, in a summer temperature that would fry
eggs on a concrete path.

Of the children, Jack, at twenty, now belonged firmly in
the grown-up class. He was fairly tall, but not as tall as
his father, thin now from strenuous work in the heat, with
a face burnt and creased by the sun. He had somewhat
bleached brown hair and strong hands, roughened and
stained with much outside work. His expression was on the
whole amiable but often tightened by worry and over-
much physical effort. His young brothers and sisters knew
better than to take too many liberties with him, but they
relied on him more than they realized.

Next came Lorna, and already her rather round face and
sturdy build seemed to give her more substance than her
mother had. Her normally quiet and serious face, if it
lacked the frequent shadows of anxiety, also lacked the
recurring twinkle of her mother's. But of them all she was
the kindest, the gentlest, and the most long-suffering.

Edward was thin, sandy haired, and very like his mother.
He was also somewhat disposed to freckles and suffered
from a spasmodically enlarged sense of responsibility. This
curbed a normal exuberance of spirits and sometimes made
him appear older than his years. Linda—or Belinda, to give
her the baptismal name her father now decreed was to be
used—and Robbie, respectively ten and nine years old, led
the most carefree lives of them all. Belinda was pretty in a
curly pink-and-white kind of way and was more gregarious

by nature than the others. Her main quarrel with correspondence lessons was that she could not do them in the
company of other little girls. Otherwise, they sat lightly on
her shoulders. Robbie, darker complexioned than Edward
and with more of a sparkle, was usually absorbed and busy
out in the paddocks or about the outbuildings.

As for Fanny, no one ever knew exactly what went on
behind those wide, noncommittal blue eyes. She led her
own quiet and secret life, and the deeps that she appeared
to inhabit were ruffled not at all by the periodical family
storms that raged over her head.

Presently Lorna put down her cup and said, "Listen!"
They held their breath, and in the silence a distant purr
came faintly through the window.

"It's him," said Jack. "I'll go and open the horse paddock
gate." Subconsciously, Lorna hoped there were no snakes,
for they sometimes came up to the house for water, and the
overgrown old garden attracted them from everywhere.
She collected the cups and put them in the sink. Then
she went out onto the veranda. There was a transparency
in the darkness now, and away to the east the sky held the
first faint promise of day. Seeing it, she felt reassured.

The sound of the motor came more clearly now, and she
could see the lights flashing and dipping as the doctor's
Austin rode the bumps. There was a movement behind her,
and she turned. Her father stood in the doorway, peering
out.

"He's coming," she said. "How's Mum, Dad?"

"Eh?" said her father vaguely. "Oh, fine, fine." But his
eyes did not leave the flickering car lights.

Doctor Roberts, when he arrived, did not look as if he
had been dragged untimely from his bed. He smiled pleas-

antly at Lorna and then disappeared inside with her father. Lorna and Jack sat down on the edge of the veranda and waited. Little by little the sky lightened. The east turned pink, then apricot, and the first streaks of sunshine tipped the crests of the hills. Lorna's head suddenly jerked, and she realized she had nearly dropped off to sleep. Now that the day had come and the time for sleep had passed, she found it was what she wanted to do more than anything. She turned to look at Jack. His knees were clasped loosely in his arms, his head had dropped forward, and he was asleep. Lorna settled herself more comfortably, leaned herself against the veranda post, and closed her eyes.

It seemed to her that they had been closed only a moment when the sound of footsteps woke her, and she and Jack sprang up, both feeling a little guilty.

Doctor Roberts looked at them both and smiled. "Your mother will cook many a leg of mutton for you yet," he said. "We're going to fix her up as good as new!" He walked briskly out to his car, and as he drove off across the paddock, it was no longer necessary to use the lights.

Mrs. Barker had been ordered to spend the day in bed—an unprecedented occurrence. When the two girls brought in her breakfast, all the rest of the family trooped in with them. "What's up, Mum?" asked Robbie, flinging himself with a bounce onto the end of the bed.

"Get off, you muttonhead; Mum's sick," said Edward angrily and jerked him off by the ankle. There was a scuffle as Robbie hit the floor.

"If you boys can't even stop brawling when your mother's lying there sick, I'll take you outside and tan the hide off the pair of you," shouted Mr. Barker with rather unnecessary violence.

"O.K., Dad. We've stopped," said Edward, who had learned just how seriously to take his father's sudden rages.

There was silence for a few moments while everyone watched Mrs. Barker begin her breakfast. Then Mr. Barker suddenly said, "Your mother's got to go to Sydney and have an operation."

"Some time," said Mrs. Barker, smiling at him.

"Not some time at all," said Mr. Barker. "As soon as we can arrange it. Doctor Roberts said those attacks would go on getting worse until you've had it, and by George, you're going to have it!" He looked fiercely at his wife from beneath a pair of eyebrows that matched his flowing white mustache.

"I think you ought to, Mum," said Jack, who had been told something of the doctor's advice by his father. "You've got to have it sooner or later, you know. And much better sooner." But he didn't sound very happy as he said it.

"Well, I don't want to go now," said Mrs. Barker. "I don't feel ill enough to want to go now, and you know quite well I couldn't possibly get away now, with all Edward's name tapes still to sew on and then Robbie and Belinda's correspondence school. I can't just drop everything like that, you know."

"You can, and you will," said Mr. Barker robustly. "Edward can sew on his own name tapes, or Lorna can. And I'll take on the correspondence myself. If you can manage it, I suppose I can."

Mrs. Barker smiled at the thought of Mr. Barker controlling his temper through a long day's correspondence school. But he went on: "And what's more, you'll have the whole treatment Doctor Roberts advised—as long as they'll keep you in hospital, and at least a month at Manly or Terrigal or somewhere else by the sea afterwards." He folded his arms in a very decisive manner.

But his wife did not appear unduly impressed. "That's a long time away from home, and not even Lorna to cook for you because she'll be at school."

"There's me," interrupted Belinda indignantly.

"Of course. And you'd do it very nicely, too. But you're not going to have to. The idea! At ten years old!"

"Nearly eleven," said Belinda promptly.

"Well, eleven. But there's another thing none of you seems to have thought of: the money. All that would cost a fortune. You've no idea how much it costs now to have an operation—unless you haven't any money at all, and then they put you in a public ward. Otherwise, it's only for rich people."

"You leave the money to me," said Mr. Barker in a lordly way.

"Well, I know we haven't got it, and I'm certainly not going on borrowed money. If this drought gets any worse you'll need every penny you can raise to buy feed for the winter. There's no need for me to go immediately, and I'm not going. Some day when it's easier to manage, we'll think about it again. In the meantime, none of you are to worry about me. I'm perfectly all right."

Mrs. Barker got up, as she had said she would, the next day, and everything went on as usual. She appeared to have recovered completely, though she did not look any less tired toward the end of the summer. Having taken her for granted all their lives, the children now began to look at her more carefully. They began to notice just how much she did in the day, how seldom she sat down and rested, and how little she ate to accomplish what she did. They had never, of course, seen anyone do less, for until they went to boarding school, they had never been anywhere much, or wanted to, being perfectly contented at home. But it seemed to them now that she was overworking. And another thing, too, began to worry them.

2: Hatching the Plot

Edward and Robbie had gone up to feed the rabbit pack, that is, the ill-assorted collection of dogs used to keep the rabbits down, for it was a Sunday and the rabbiter didn't turn up on weekends. Belinda and Lorna were coming back from shutting the fowls up for the night and collecting the eggs, with Fanny, as usual, in tow. They met at the stockyards and, as there was no particular hurry, somehow came to a stop there. It was a warm, still summer afternoon, and at half-past six the sun still shone with more than a trace of its midday heat. Between the stockyards and the house, where all the sheds stood, the dry earth was beaten to a fine dust by the passage of many feet and hooves, and the least breeze, or the passage of a mob of sheep, would lift it into the air, where it hung like a pall for perhaps an hour or so.

The smell of dust in their nostrils was so constant during these months that it would not have seemed like summer without it. This year, in particular, there was rather more than usual because there had been so little rain.

The sheds consisted of the usual collection of outhouses —a machinery shed, shearing shed, shearers' quarters, hay shed, cow stalls, and a couple of tall cylindrical galvanized iron silos for storing grain. At the moment these last were three parts empty, for the oat crop in the spring had not been a success. With the exception of the silos, which were fairly new, all the sheds were badly in need of repair. Doors sagged at their hinges, roofing iron flapped loose at the corners, and many of the timber supports were quite obviously feeling the pressure of sheer old age. Mr. Barker regarded these repairs as wet-weather jobs; the only trouble was that there were more jobs than wet weather, and maintenance kept getting a longer and longer lead on him as time went on.

To the west beyond the stockyards, the ground fell away toward the river in open paddocks, and now from this deep cleft in the hills the first faintly cooler breaths of air came up in little puffs.

By common, though silent, consent, the children put down their tins and buckets and climbed onto the top rail of the fence, where they had the advantage both of the slightly increased air movement and the view. Only Fanny, her everlasting blue jeans having at this stage of the day taken on a sort of gray protective coloring, sat herself down in the softest and therefore the deepest patch of dust she could find and thereupon became almost invisible.

No one said anything for a few minutes. They let the heat and effort of the day drain out of them. From the calf

pen one of the calves, shut away from its mother for the
night, blared indignantly, and from a distant hillside came
the bleat of a sheep on its way to spend the night at the
sheep camp at the top.

Then Robbie pointed down the hill and said, "That's
where we had our party—the big tree you can see the top
of."

"Doesn't it seem ages," said Belinda. "It's not so long
ago, really."

Lorna nodded. "It was two nights after that Mum got
sick."

"Know what I think?" said Edward. "I reckon it was
our party that did it."

"Oh, Edward," said Belinda. "You don't think there was
something bad, do you? And we were so careful to put the
sausages in the refrigerator, weren't we, Lorna?"

"Edward doesn't mean sick 'on the stummick,'" said
Lorna, who hadn't listened to the conversation of Charlie
the rabbiter for nothing. "Do you, Edward?"

"I think she worked too hard," said Edward. "That's
what."

"Oh," said Belinda and pondered.

Robbie said with sudden, defensive loudness, "I worked
too hard, too—by jings!—I worked that night!"

Edward looked at him with some scorn. "Shut up," he
said briefly.

Lorna, with a frown creasing her forehead, looked up
and said, "Do you really, Edward?"

Edward nodded. "Don't you?" he asked.

Before she could answer, Belinda said in an anguished
sort of screech, "But we did just *everything* for Mum at
the party. We promised we would and we did. How could

she be so tired it made her sick when we made the puddings and did the plates and mugs and helped her with the turkey and—and all?"

"She certainly was tired. Yes, I suppose I do," Lorna said to Edward, apparently having failed to hear Belinda's remark. This was a habit of her elder sister and brother that annoyed Belinda exceedingly.

Now her face became suffused and she shouted, "I say we did all the work! Can't you hear? She wasn't tired. She couldn't be."

"I can hear you, Lindy," said Robbie who, having just been rebuffed himself, sensed an ally in his equally down-trodden sister. His tone had been particularly winning, but it met with a startling and unexpected response.

She leaned over and gave him a push that was meant to, but didn't quite, unseat him. "Call me Belinda! And get away, you silly thing," she said furiously. Then she shouted at Lorna again: "I don't want Mum to have an operation because of the party. I don't want it to have been our fault." The muscles of her chin contracted, and her eyes began to glisten.

This time Lorna appeared to hear her. "None of us do," she said. "But it won't just *not* be because we don't *want* it to. It was just after the party she got sick, you know."

"Can't see it was anything else," said Edward gloomily. "What else happened just before except the party? Nothing. So it was all our fault."

They all digested this, unpalatable as it was. Then Belinda said meekly, "What can we do to make up?"

"I'll give her my fox skin Charlie gave me," said Robbie. "She loves that, and the smell's nearly gone now."

Edward shook his head absently. He was thinking. He said slowly, "There's only one thing Mum needs."

"I know," said Lorna. "Money."

"I've got two and sevenpence," said Belinda. "Left from the show."

"I've got some pennies and two sixpences," said Robbie.

"I've got ten shillings left over from last term's pocket money," said Lorna.

"That's thirteen and something," said Edward. "That won't go far, and I haven't got any. I went and bought that stuff for the pups. Wish I hadn't."

There was a long silence.

Then Lorna said, "I wish we could make some."

"Couldn't we?" said Belinda. "Oh, couldn't we, Lorna?"

"How?" asked Edward.

"Well, couldn't we—couldn't we all *do* something? Together, I mean." Belinda's gloom vanished. She was now full of enthusiasm.

"How can we?" said Lorna. "Edward and I'll be at school soon."

"Do we have to make it together?" said Edward. "Could we all just make what we can during the term and see what we've got next holidays?"

"It seems a long time to wait, with Mum sick," said Lorna. She thought for a while. "Still, perhaps it's better than nothing."

"How'll we make it?" asked Robbie. "Perhaps I could sell my fox skin."

"Everyone has to think out his own way," said Edward, whose mind was now working more quickly. "We got to get the money because it was our fault, and we don't want Mum sick anyway. And if we collect a big lot—somehow

—and give it to her and say it isn't borrowed and it's specially for the operation, she'll just feel she's got to use it."
He paused, and they all felt this reasoning to be unanswerable. He looked around at them, the gloom somewhat lifted
from his face. "What say we do it? Shall we?"

"I'll do anything," said Lorna more soberly, "so that we
can get Mum fixed up. It's terrible she got sick doing something for us." Fortunately, it did not occur to her that almost every one of Mrs. Barker's multitudinous activities
involved doing something for them. "I don't know what I
can do, but I'll think of something."

"So'll I," said Belinda. "I might get Sadie to sell something for me. She got two shillings for a fountain pen she
found on the footpath once. It didn't have a top, either. She
told me."

Edward snorted. His opinion of Belinda's friend Sadie
was not high. She had been asked to the party against his
wish.

"I'm going to borrow Dad's shotgun and go shooting
dingoes," said Robbie. "Charlie says there's more money in
dingoes than rabbits."

"Since when have you been using Dad's shotgun?" asked
Edward suspiciously, for this was his own dearest wish.

"Oh well," said Robbie. "For a real job like that, he
might let me."

"We've got to think of real things," said Lorna. "Pretend things are no good." She looked at Robbie rather
anxiously, for she knew it was sometimes hard to get him
down from his castles in the air.

But Robbie said indignantly, "Dingoes aren't pretend
things."

"But your using the shotgun is," said Edward. "You got to be sensible about this. You got to really *try*."

"I am," said Robbie furiously. "I've thought of two things already. And what have *you* thought of?" As Edward hadn't yet the slightest idea how he was to make any money at boarding school, he wasn't able to reply.

But now Lorna glanced around, saw that the sun, a dazzling red ball, was almost on the horizon, and hopped off the fence. A little swirl of dust came up around her as she landed. "Come on," she said. "We'd better go and help Mum get tea now, anyway."

They all jumped down, each descending into a thicker cloud of dust. "We'll all begin from now," Lorna said, "and see who gets the most by next holidays. We can tell each other what we're doing if we want to."

"But don't tell anyone else," said Edward. "We got to keep it secret, or some silly coot'll get the idea we ought to be doing something else instead or that Dad ought to collect our money or something. It always happens."

No one questioned the truth of this statement. They knew it was all too true.

"What about Fan?" said Belinda in a loud whisper.

They all glanced around, but Fanny was in a distant corner of the yard and was making a pattern with the new-laid eggs in the dust. She seemed to have forgotten they existed.

They had no further opportunity to discuss the plan, but it was in the minds of them all. That evening Mrs. Barker found them excessively willing but unusually absentminded. Where Lorna and Edward were concerned, she put it down to the thought of school. She wondered, a little anxiously, how Edward would get on at boarding school. Lorna had not minded, or at least had not said she minded, but Edward was much more of a home lover. He had always been like the bush children she had known farther west in her young days, who were inclined to run and hide at the sight of a stranger. Edward had a habit of vanishing unobtrusively, too, at the sight of a strange car. But she realized that she would never know how he felt, for he would never tell her.

It was not easy for Mr. and Mrs. Barker to send all their children, one by one, to boarding school, but the alternative was such a complicated arrangement of buses and such hours of traveling every day to get to and from the nearest big town that they had decided against it.

Besides, as Mr. Barker with unaccustomed modesty had said to his wife, "I'll never be able to leave 'em much when I go. I never was a good provider, and I don't suppose I ever will be now. Best I can do is to leave 'em with well-trained brains, and that's something that will stick by 'em till they die."

From the time Jack was born, Mrs. Barker had been quietly saving what she could. Although she had not said so, this was the main reason behind her refusal to go to the hospital. Mr. Barker understood her reasons, but no one else did.

That night as Lorna was just dropping off to sleep, she felt her bed give a little lurch. Her eyes flew open, but it was only Belinda who bent over her and now hissed in her ear, "Here's my money. I counted it. It's two and ninepence, really. That's pretty good, isn't it?"

"Well, it's better than two and sevenpence," said Lorna. "What are you going to do with it?"

"Give it to you," said Belinda.

"It's not much good my having it," said Lorna. "I won't be here."

"Well, someone's got to have it," said Belinda. "And I think the eldest ought to."

"Oh well," said Lorna, who was feeling an urgent need for sleep. "Put it under my pillow for tonight, and we'll have a meeting about it in the morning."

She felt Belinda's hand slide beneath her ear and heard the muffled jingle of coins. She went to sleep with the comfortable feeling that the foundation, at any rate, had been laid.

The meeting next day took place behind the henhouse. Like other conspirators, they found that one of the chief drawbacks to conspiring was the lack of a place to meet where they could be private. Once Mrs. Barker had fed the fowls, a job she liked to do herself in the mornings, the henhouse was safe enough, provided they didn't startle the hens into cackling—an occurrence that was very likely to send Mrs. Barker hurrying down with a shotgun under her arm. She defended her fowls against crows, snakes, or foxes with considerable ferocity. They left Fanny behind, remembering that one of her favorite forms of sport was catching unsuspecting fowls by the tail. She was particularly good at this, and the other children said it was because she had the evil eye.

They had to creep away unobtrusively one at a time and now sat side by side leaning against the henhouse wall. The sun blazed down on them, but they screwed up their eyes against the glare and ignored it.

"What's up?" said Edward in a hushed voice.

"Nothing, but we haven't decided what to do with the money we get." Lorna held out her hand, disclosing Belinda's two and ninepence. "There's this, and it's not much good my having it."

"It's pretty important, minding money," said Edward solemnly. "We can't let just anybody have it." If his glance passed over Belinda and Robbie as he said it, it was with so light a touch that they failed to notice it.

"I know," said Robbie. "Jack."

There was a pause. Then Edward shook his head. "I reckon we don't tell Jack at all," he said.

"But think all Jack'll save," said Belinda, who was a trifle mercenary. "He gets a wage."

"He wouldn't give it to us, though," said Lorna practically. "Jack's too grown up. We mustn't tell him. He wouldn't mean to, but he'd spoil it."

Edward nodded. "We got to think of a hiding place. That's the only thing."

"Grownups put their money in banks," said Belinda.

Edward looked at her with scorn. "How do you think you're going to get to a bank without anyone's seeing you?" he asked. "It wouldn't be a secret long."

"I know," said Lorna. "Let's take Jack's old Meccano box. Nobody ever plays with it now, and anyway most of the pieces have gone."

"That's a good idea," said Edward. "We can use that and keep it under that loose floorboard in my room."

"Be better under my bed," said Belinda. "Where I can watch it when you've gone to school."

This idea appealed neither to Edward nor to Robbie, and they were going to protest forcibly when there was a sudden panic of fluttering on the other side of the wall behind them, and all the hens started cackling on a shrill note of indignation and fear. The conspirators leapt to their feet

as one man and were poised for flight when a shadow fell across the ground at one end of the wall—a short, round shadow—and Fanny came sidling around the corner. If she was pleased she had found them, she gave no sign of it. She gazed at them balefully for perhaps half a minute and then withdrew, and as soon as she disappeared, the hens, whose cackles had simmered down to a prolonged and less hysterical protest, broke out again in frenzy.

"Come on," said Edward. "No good staying here any longer, and we've got to take her away from those hens before Mum hears."

"Bet she's put them off their lay already," said Robbie with a joyful glint in his eye. He knew better than to go to Fanny's assistance in whatever it was she was doing, but he was sorely tempted.

They strolled around the corner of the henhouse, and Lorna and Edward, with the practiced motion of persons

with long experience, bore down on Fanny, who still had a few of the hens bailed up in one corner, grasped her by the arms, and dragged her out. She shut her mouth tight, for she was not given to screaming, but her face became suffused with purple, and she lashed out savagely with her feet. Edward and Lorna had her at arm's length, but even so they grunted from time to time as her shoes connected with their defenseless legs.

"Savage, isn't she?" said Robbie in an interested way as he walked beside them. " 'Minds me of that last milker Jack broke in, except she had horns."

"Fan'll have horns one day," said Edward between his teeth. "After she's dead."

Halfway to the house Mrs. Barker met them, and the shotgun was under her arm. "Oh, it's you," she said. "I thought it must have been a snake. What's happened?"

A glance flashed between Lorna and Edward, and Lorna said, "Fan."

"That's funny," said Mrs. Barker, looking at her youngest daughter as if she were an entomological specimen. "She doesn't usually go down there on her own. What were the rest of you doing there?"

"Oh, we—we were just strolling past," said Belinda unconvincingly.

"I see," said Mrs. Barker, and they knew quite well she didn't see at all. However, she only added, "You can let Fan go now. She won't go down again."

Edward and Lorna dropped her arms so that she sat down rather suddenly. She rose and, after one glowering look at each of them, walked with dignity over to her mother and took a piece of her skirt in one dirty hand.

They all returned together, peculiar feelings of guilt silencing the other four children. They were beginning to realize that all clandestine schemes, however virtuous, are apt to be misunderstood.

Later in the day, when the opportunity presented itself, they gathered around the old tin Meccano box. The bits of Meccano and other types of building metal that had been collected with the years were discarded. Lorna wiped it out with a damp cloth and discovered that the paint was not gray but green. Then Belinda, with considerable ceremony, laid her two and ninepence in it.

"Never mind," said Edward. "It'll look more when there's some other money beside it."

"I'll get mine," said Lorna and went off to fetch her ten shillings. "Mum'll wonder why I have to have a whole new two pounds for school this time," she said as she dropped in the note.

"I wonder should you?" said Edward, for there seemed a lack of logic here, though he could not put his finger on it.

"How are we ever going to collect enough if we don't put in what we have?" asked Belinda, and for the moment this seemed sufficient answer.

Then Robbie came with his and said as he let it fall in with a pleasant tinkle, "Fan's got some pennies, too. She keeps them in a matchbox. Why shouldn't she put hers in, too?"

"She ought to," said Belinda. "Look at all Mum has to do for her."

"Go and get it, Rob," said Edward.

Robbie brought the matchbox, but unfortunately just as he was opening it to extract the pennies, Fanny came into the room. Wherever she had been, she must have seen him take the box, for she had her eyes on it now. As he took out the pennies, she rushed at him, grabbing at his arm, and, this once, opened her mouth and screeched. In his surprise Robbie dropped the pennies. He and Fanny bobbed down to pick them up and bumped their heads. Tears began to stream down Fanny's contorted face. They heard Mrs. Barker's quickly approaching footsteps, and Edward swiftly shut the Meccano box and pushed it under the quilt.

"Whatever's the matter?" said Mrs. Barker as she came into the room. "What's happened to Fanny?" She saw her on the floor by the bed, saw the moist and anguished face, and quickly picked her up. "What made her scream?" she asked the others, for it was an unusual enough occurrence to cause comment.

For a moment no one answered. They looked at Fanny, who now had three of the pennies clutched in her hand. But Fanny said nothing, only opened her hand, gazed at the coins, and then bent over her mother's arm and began searching the floor. Mrs. Barker could not help seeing the money in her hand. "Whose is this?" she asked.

Lorna swallowed. "Fan's," she said.

"Did you give them to her?"

"No," said Lorna. "She—she just had them. She kept—keeps—them in a matchbox."

Mrs. Barker looked more serious than she usually did. "Then what are they doing all over the floor?"

Lorna looked at Robbie, but the words failed her. Then Robbie, who had some more of the pennies in his hand and still knelt on the floor, looked his mother in the face and said, "I took them, Mum."

"I told him to," said Edward quickly.

"We didn't think she ought to have them," said Belinda.

"But why not?" asked Mrs. Barker.

"Well, we—she—doesn't really know what money's for," said Lorna, finishing in a burst as inspiration came to her.

But it did not seem like inspiration to Mrs. Barker. Her face became grave as she said, "You were taking Fanny's pennies away from her?"

"Yes, Mum," said three humble voices.

"Well, give them back, please, and I hope that none of you will ever, ever take anybody's money again."

Mrs. Barker walked out of the room, and they could hear her footsteps disappearing down the passage toward the kitchen. It was not her usual brisk step.

A gulp came from Belinda. "I think we should tell Mum," she said in a quavering voice.

Edward turned on her angrily. "Don't you dare!" he said. "Mum'll know one day—when we're dead, maybe— and she'll be sorry she thought we were thieves." He took the remainder of the pennies from Robbie. "Here, Fan, you go now."

There was silence as they watched Fanny, matchbox in hand, strut toward the door. Without a backward glance, and every so often shaking the pennies so that they rattled, she followed her mother down the polished linoleum of the passageway.

"Oh dear," said Lorna with a sigh. "It doesn't seem fair, does it?"

Mrs. Barker said no more about the incident, and they were fairly sure that she had told neither Mr. Barker nor Jack; yet they knew that she was still wondering and puzzling and was not very happy about what she had seen. It was difficult to resist the temptation to tell her everything.

Even Lorna showed signs of weakening, but Edward was adamant and insisted that once they told a single soul they would, somehow or other, be made to give up their scheme.

"They'll think it's just a kid's thing and spoil it. But it's real. Isn't it? *Isn't* it?" He gave them each a searching look, and they could only agree and put their weakness aside.

3: Brigalow

When it came to the point, it was not easy to think of any plan that involved actually making money. It was all very well to put what money they already had into the Meccano box, but it amounted only to something under a pound, and Edward told them they would need a hundred pounds at least.

For a long time none of them could think of any way at all to earn even a few shillings. Robbie thought they might have offered their services to their father for something under the basic wage, but Lorna pointed out that to make money by taking it from the family was not at all a practical approach. Belinda, inspired by a visit she had once paid

to a Bungaree concert, thought they might act, sing, or
dance something together. The others were quite horrified
at this idea and begged her not to think of it again. And now
the holidays were running out. When there was only a
week left, Edward said to Belinda and Robbie, "You're
not to forget about it when we're gone, now. Promise?
Lorna and I will go on thinking at school, and you've got
to, too."

"We will," they told him. "We promise. Cut our throat
and spit our death!"

The conversation took place at the dog kennels; the kennels, that is, for the sheep dogs, not the rabbit pack, which
ranked pretty low in the canine social grades. The sheep
dogs all had individual owners and were expected to obey
and remain faithful to their owners at all times. Nothing
of this sort was expected of the rabbit pack, whose sole
duty in life was to chase and kill rabbits. Mr. Barker and
Jack had several dogs of their own. Lorna had had one, but
it was now in the not very successful process of being
adopted by Belinda. Robbie and Fanny were considered
too young to have dogs, for every dog owner in the Barker
family had to feed and train his own dog. But Edward,
besides Spicer, whom he had had for many years and who
was not strictly speaking a sheep dog, had one Border collie
bitch of his own. This bitch had proved too timid to be
of much practical use. She cringed if another dog was
scolded, she ran for cover if too many people started shouting at once, and as soon as anyone used a stockwhip she
went home. So Edward had been allowed to breed from
her, and she was now the happy mother of a half-grown
family of four.

George Trevor, the eldest son of their next-door neighbor, owned the father. He was a dog with a long pedigree and a reputation for intelligent work that George maintained was rather less than the truth. Even making allowances for the opinion of a proud owner, he was a dog of considerable prowess, and Edward had been very shy of asking that a mating might take place with his little bitch. Eventually Jack had asked for him, and George had agreed very readily, only stipulating that he might have one of the puppies.

This he now had, having chosen it himself from the litter when they were trotting about strongly, their tails still erect little whips and their extended middles like small balloons with the soft pink skin showing through on the under side. Now they were half grown, at their most uncoordinated and ill-proportioned, with big feet and uncontrolled legs, and full of a misguided and undisciplined exuberance. George was satisfied that he had taken the pick of them, but Edward, who had spent many hours of every day with them since they were born, was convinced that the most promising still remained with him. He christened him Brigalow and under Jack's instructions had been training him for months.

He had originally started off on his own, and Jack had come across him making off to the paddock where the wether weaners were kept, with Brigalow bounding and racing, not exactly with but fairly near him.

"Where are you off to?" asked Jack.

"Going to start training my dog," said Edward importantly.

Jack shifted his hat and scratched his head. "I see," he said noncommittally. "Where were you thinking of training him?"

"Thought I'd practice on the wether weaners," said Edward. "They'll be nice and lively—give him a run."

"He'll give them a run, I should think!" said Jack. "Know how you're going to stop him once he gets started?"

"Oh, he mostly comes when I call him," said Edward airily.

"Not when he gets started after sheep he won't," said Jack. "Not if you haven't taught him first."

"Oh, but he likes me," said Edward. "I know he'll come."

At that moment a little group of sheep under a nearby tree saw them, raised their heads with a jerk, and started to canter off to a less populated part of the paddock. Brigalow, trotting in a carefree manner a little way ahead, saw them, too. He stopped and watched them, ears pricked, tail quivering, and one front paw raised. Then, like a streak he was off. Edward and Jack heard the little yaps of excitement he gave as he raced after the sheep. They heard them, too, and increased their pace.

"Here, Brig," called Edward. "Here, boy!" But Brigalow raced on.

"Here, Brig! Brig! Brig!" shouted Edward as loudly as his vocal cords would allow. "Come back here at once." It seemed impossible that the dog should not have heard him, but he gave no indication of having done so. He was among the sheep now, barking and bounding, and they spread fanwise before him, panic-stricken and panting.

"See what I mean?" said Jack. "Now you'll have to catch him, and then you'll have to scold him, and then he'll think he mustn't chase sheep, but his instinct will tell him he must, and so he'll end up a nasty mixed-up mess."

"Oh jings!" said Edward. "What'll I do?"

"Go and catch him now before he's run them quite to death, and then I'll tell you," said Jack. He waited while Edward sped off, still calling loudly to his oblivious dog.

It took Edward some time to catch Brigalow because every time he started to run after him, the dog thought he was joining in the delightful new game and pursued the bewildered sheep all the harder. But eventually he caught up with him, grabbed his collar, and, unbuckling his belt, ran it through the keeper. After Jack's words he did not know whether to scold or praise, so they returned in silence to where Jack was now squatting in the shade of a tree.

"What you've got to do," said Jack—and his words now fell on more than willing ears—"is to teach him to obey you before he ever gets near the sheep. He's sure to want to chase them. That's because he's a sheep dog. But don't give him the chance till you know you can stop him."

"How?" said Edward.

"Start with teaching him two things: to get behind and to sit. You can do it by having him on a chain to start with. Tell him to do it, and then pull him till he does. If you do it a few times, he'll soon learn."

"Good-o," said Edward. "And when I've taught him that, what then?"

Jack looked at him and grinned. "When you've taught him that, you come to me." He climbed to his feet, picked up his bridle, and continued his interrupted way to catch his horse.

Edward and Brigalow went home. And for many days after that Brigalow was given lessons number one and two. There were times when he seemed to be learning with sweet docility everything that he should, and there were others when he only wished to play, refused to concentrate, and would persist in bounding and barking around Edward's feet until Edward began to think he did not, after all, have a brain in his head.

Sometimes Jack would come upon them in a quiet place behind one of the sheds, or away down the paddock, and would watch the performance carefully, advising, warning, or encouraging as the need arose. Edward was thankful when he took the time to do this, for Jack's dogs were models of efficiency and obedience, and there was no doubt that he knew what he was talking about.

One day when Brigalow had been particularly exasperating Edward handed the end of the chain to Jack.

"Here," he said. "You do it. I might be doing it wrong."

But Jack shook his head. "I can't," he said. "He's got to be taught to obey you, not me. You're his boss. Of course, if you'd like to *give* him to me—"

"No thanks," said Edward quickly. "I'll do it, then." And he tried once more.

Another day when Jack happened very fortunately to be there, Brigalow was more obtuse than usual, and Edward lost his temper. He shouted at him and picked up a stick and was about to bring it down on Brigalow's back when Jack said, "Hold on!"

Edward stopped, Brigalow's chain in one hand and the stick upraised in the other.

"Don't do that," said Jack.

"Why not?" said Edward, panting a little with rage rather than exertion. "He's not even trying. You can see. I got to punish him."

He raised the stick again. But Jack said quietly, "No, you haven't. You only want to."

There was a silence. Then Edward slowly lowered the stick. "Yes," he said. "That's right." He took a deep breath, threw the stick away, and quietly repeated the lesson.

"Losing your temper and doing something silly only muddles him and maybe frightens him. Then you'll have to start from the beginning or even farther back. Training a dog's training yourself, too, you know. It's not all that easy." Brigalow had just come behind as he was told, and Jack put a hand on his head. "You're both learning," he said. "We'll have him out among the sheep before you go off to school."

This had happened perhaps a week before the conversation at the kennels, and Jack had not been present on any subsequent occasion. By now all the puppies were tied up to their own kennels, and feeding his pack of five kept Edward busy. He knew that some day he would have to get rid of at least two others, but so far he had not been able to bring himself to think about it. He was extremely proud of the whole litter and entertained a secret hope that he might hit on a reason for keeping them all.

"Which is Brigalow?" asked Belinda, who could never tell one horse or dog from another.

"That one, stupid," said Robbie, pointing. "Let's see you work him, Edward."

"He's not working yet," said Edward. "But I think I've got him trained good. Like to see?" He stood the feed tin on a post and let the dog go.

He let him run for a time and then gave him, one by one, the orders he had been trying for so long to teach him. Twice he went through them, and each time Brigalow did as he was told, immediately and without question.

A voice from the nearby machinery shed said, "Good for

you. We'll take him out in the paddock now the next time I've got a minute." And they saw that Jack had been watching the whole performance from a reclining position beneath the tractor.

Edward looked exceedingly pleased, but all he said was, "You better make it soon, then. I haven't got too long."

It was the next afternoon that Jack decided he had some time to spare, and he and Edward, with Brigalow and Jack's own dog walking demurely behind, went off to find some sheep.

"What if he chases them again?" said Edward.

"We won't give him a chance this time," said Jack. "We'll arrange it so he brings them."

Edward did not know quite what he meant, but it very soon became clear when Jack's dog obligingly rounded up a small mob of sheep for them, and Jack told Edward that he was always to stay on the opposite side of the sheep from the dog. This, Edward discovered, involved a great deal of running, and often at high speed, but it also meant that whenever Brigalow tried to join him, he was forced to bring the mob of sheep as well. Once or twice, between them, they scattered the sheep, and then Jack would give a whistle and his own dog would gather them again. He would whistle again, and the dog would flop to the ground wherever he happened to be, his tongue lolling and his sides heaving.

"Couldn't I do it by whistle?" asked Edward, for he much admired his brother's technique.

"You could," said Jack, "if you could whistle loud enough. But can you?"

Edward blew his cheeks out, pursed his lips and inadvertently crossed his eyes, and did his best to copy Jack's expert sounds, but his were very windy affairs, and Jack shook his head. "You've got to whistle with your tongue on the top of your mouth. Doing it with your lips isn't loud enough." He demonstrated, and his dog leapt up and waited expectantly. "You'll have to stick to voice now with Brig. But if you can get out a good whistle, you can probably get him used to it later."

They continued the training, and before they left the paddock later in the afternoon, Brigalow showed signs that he was beginning to grasp what was expected of him. He ceased to gambol madly up to the sheep and developed a habit of stalking and watching them more quietly, waiting to see which way they intended to run before darting off in pursuit. He obviously enjoyed his work, but to Edward's annoyance he appeared equally pleased with himself whether he did it well or badly. However, Jack looked satisfied and said, as they tied the dogs up to their kennels again, "He'll be all right. You'll see. We'll give him a few more goes before you leave, and he'll do then until you come back."

Jack said much the same thing at supper that night. He and his father had been talking, and Edward, who had not been listening very carefully, heard him say, "That dog of Edward's is showing some promise, Dad. He'll be all right when he has a bit more age on him."

"Glad to hear it," said Mr. Barker. "We need a few more dogs coming on. That reminds me. I meant to tell you, I was talking to Murphy in town the other day, and he told me he just sold a likely sort of sheep dog for fifty pounds."

"That's a lot of money," said Jack thoughtfully. He glanced at Edward, but his eyes were on his plate, although

he appeared to be eating rather slowly. Lorna, Belinda, and
Robbie had stopped eating and were looking at their father.

"*How* much?" asked Robbie in an incredulous squeak.

"Fifty pounds," said Mr. Barker. "Or it may have been
guineas. I forget."

Silence greeted this statement, but three pairs of eyes
found one another, looked hard, and then returned to the
plates in front of them.

Later on, Lorna, Belinda, and Robbie gathered around
Edward. "Edward, did you hear what Dad said?" asked
Belinda in an excited whisper.

"Fifty pounds," said Lorna slowly. "It's a lot of money."

"That was for a trained dog," said Edward shortly.

"Brig's nearly trained, Edward," said Belinda.

"Imagine getting fifty pounds!" said Robbie.

Lorna looked carefully at Edward and then said, "But
of course he isn't *properly* trained yet, is he?"

Edward looked around at them all, and he was frowning
horribly. For a moment he did not speak. Then he said in a
voice different from his usual one, "I'll bet they were
pedigree ones. They'd never pay that for a dog that didn't
have a pedigree on *both* sides. Mine's only got a pedigree on
one." He turned and walked quickly away.

The others stood in a little silent group and watched him
go. Then Belinda said, "Well, if he can get all that money
for one dog, I think he ought to. Even if Brig only has half
a pedigree and the man only pays half as much, it's still an
awful lot of money, isn't it, Rob?"

"Terrible lot," said Robbie with his eyes popping. "I bet
I'd ring Murphy up if I was Edward. I bet I'd take Brig in
tonight, even. Imagine having all that money in the Meccano box!"

"Edward's terribly fond of Brig," said Lorna thought-fully.

"He's got Spicer, hasn't he?" said the only dogless member of the group with some bitterness.

"Spicer's not the same, Robbie," said Lorna. "He didn't have him from a pup, and he never trained him."

"Well, I think Mum's more important than any dog," said Belinda, who regarded animals of any kind with only modified rapture.

"I know," said Lorna. She paused and then said, "I'm glad I'm not Edward, that's all."

No more was said on the subject at that time, but there was at least one member of the conspirators who was unable to forget it.

All too soon the last days of the holidays came and, alas, went. Lorna and Edward put the final things in their suitcases and cleaned the shoes they were to wear. Not the least of Edward's troubles was that his shoes were new. He detested new clothes, and his suitcase, as he well knew, was full of them.

Mrs. Barker appeared to be as well as she usually was and, in her going-to-town clothes on the morning of their departure, looked fresh and pleasing. Lorna and Edward, with their plans scarcely begun and the long term's absence ahead of them, both hoped privately that she would not need the money until they had managed to get it.

All the family, except Jack and Fanny, were going in to the train. Jack was taking Fanny burr-cutting with him, for she was never taken to town if it could be avoided. It made the trip pleasanter for the others. But they waited to say good-by, for it was an occasion of note when two of the children went off to boarding school at once. The luggage was already in the car, and Mr. Barker was asking the distant heavens, as he usually did, why women could never be on time, when Lorna and Edward in their school uniforms, Lorna looking faintly depressed and Edward looking furious, came around the corner of the house. Fanny, seeing them, appeared to change her mind, for she turned and trotted back past them.

" 'By, Fan," said Lorna to the disappearing blue jeans.

" 'By, Fan," echoed Edward. But Fanny was deaf and did not hear.

Then Mrs. Barker and Belinda came out. They said good-by to Jack and packed themselves into the car. Before Mr. Barker had time to put his foot on the self-starter, Fanny returned, and for once she was running. Not that her turn of speed was anything remarkable, but it showed that an effort was being made. She raced up to the car, holding out her fist first to Lorna and then to Edward. Mr. Barker started the engine, and the car leapt forward, enveloping Jack and Fanny in a cloud of dust. Lorna and Edward opened their hands as the car gathered speed across the horse paddock. A warm, damp penny lay in the palm of each.

4: The Seamstress

It was during that day in Bungaree after Lorna and Edward had left on the train that Belinda first noticed the baby shop. It had not been there long, and Belinda had not noticed it before. It sold other things besides baby clothes, for Bungaree was not a big enough town to support very specialized shops. But it was the baby clothes one noticed, for the window was full of them, laid out with much skill to catch the eye.

They caught Belinda's eye, for she enjoyed both sewing and knitting and was considered to be the sewer of the family. It was a reputation she was at some pains to retain, for it is always nice to be best at something, even if one is only best because no one else has tried very hard to do it. To please her mother, she had occasionally made baby

clothes for the Country Women's Association, the Red
Cross, or church fairs. So she took a professional interest in
these baby clothes. None of them looked beyond her
powers. She had, indeed, often done more complicated
knitting patterns and embroidery stitches herself. She wondered how much money the shop gave for them. It should
not be difficult to clothe all the newly born babies in Bungaree; there could not be more than one or two a week.

When she went into the baker's shop to buy the bread
for her mother, she was pleased to see that her friend Sadie
was back from school and behind the counter.

They greeted one another with pleasure. Each admired
the other for a variety of supposed qualities that would
have astonished their mothers.

"Gee, that was a lovely party," said Sadie. "Mum said I
was liverish all next day from what I ate."

"Oh, good," said Belinda, accepting the compliment in
the spirit in which it was offered. Then she said, "I
see there's a new baby shop in town."

"Oh, that," said Sadie. "It's been here for ages—couple
of weeks at least."

"Who runs it?" asked Belinda.

Sadie shrugged her thin little shoulders. "Some foreign
lady. She speaks funny. You can't understand her hardly."

But Belinda was not interested in her personal peculiari-
ties. "Where does she get all the clothes?" she asked. "Up
from town?"

Sadie shook her head. "Shouldn't think so. Not all, anyway. Mum heard her say to Mrs. Dowdie at church one
day how she'd heard she knitted so nice and would she like
to knit some things for her. Funny, isn't it? You'd think

people'd want to make their own baby clothes. Mum says bought ones are never so nice."

"And is she?" asked Belinda, ignoring the last part of Sadie's remark.

"What?" asked Sadie, baffled for the moment. "Having a baby? As to that I couldn't say." She looked prim.

"No, silly," said Belinda, who was not in the least interested in Mrs. Dowdie's babies and disliked Sadie when she became prim. "I mean, is she making them—the baby clothes?"

"Oh, I wouldn't know," said Sadie somewhat huffily. "Mum couldn't hear any more."

Realizing that the vein of Sadie's information was now closed, Belinda drifted off, the bread under her arm. She had a few minutes to fill in while Mrs. Barker bought Robbie some new shoes, and she strolled up to the baby-shop window again. The garments all looked extremely simple and quite small. She wondered what the woman had paid for them—pounds, probably. At any rate, there was no price on them, and her mother, Belinda remembered, had once told her that usually meant a thing was pretty expensive. Her heart beat rather faster as she considered what a contribution she might have made to their funds by the end of the term. She considered going inside and asking the foreign lady what she paid but decided that the situation might become too difficult for her to handle, particularly if the foreign lady could not be understood. She thought that the best thing to do would be to make one garment and take it in when she was in Bungaree some other day. She studied the offerings spread out so enticingly before her and decided on a jacket.

She had just made up her mind to ask her mother if she could go into the general store before they went home, to choose needles, wool, and pattern, when she remembered that she was to know nothing of the plan. It would be impossible to explain why she wanted them. She considered slipping in quickly by herself and putting them on the account but then recalled the careful scrutiny each month's account was subjected to before it was paid. An item like that would never get past without comment. With a deflated sort of feeling she realized that nothing but cash would do—a rank injustice when it was cash she was aiming to acquire. She returned home weighed down with cares, and her mother thought that she was missing Lorna and Edward.

When an opportunity offered, she discussed the problem with Robbie. He was full of gratifying admiration that she had, at least, thought of a scheme and felt that the acquiring of sufficient money to start the venture was certain to be a minor obstacle.

"Well *you* think," said Belinda with justifiable annoyance.

"Get some from Jack," said Robbie promptly. "He mostly gives it to us if we ask him."

"Well, I don't think he will this time," said Belinda. "And I bet he doesn't without asking what it's for."

"You could say you wanted to write to a shop for something," said Robbie.

"Y—yes," said Belinda doubtfully. "Except he knows I don't write well enough, and he might ask what for."

"Don't suppose he'd give you enough, anyway," said Robbie, thinking deeply. Belinda thought, too, but it was Robbie, the wicked one, who hit on the solution. Perhaps it was to Belinda's credit that she had not thought of it at all. Even he said the words in a small voice that half wished to remain unheard.

"I know where you can get the money."

This time Belinda knew he had hit on a practical solution. "Where?" she asked quickly.

His eye caught hers in one swift flash and then dropped again as he answered, "In the Meccano box."

"Robbie!" The word was forced out of her in a shocked gasp.

Robbie turned slowly and met her reproving eye. "Well?" he said defiantly. "What's wrong?"

"That'd be stealing," said Belinda.

"It's our money, isn't it?" said Robbie.

"Yes, but Lorna and Edward would say we shouldn't. You know they would."

"They're not here," said Robbie.

"I daren't," said Belinda. "Suppose I couldn't put it back?"

"Why?" said Robbie.

"She mightn't buy the coat," said Belinda.

"I mean," explained Robbie, "why suppose? Supposing's silly."

Belinda, in desperation, decided on underhand tactics. "You're too small," she said. "You don't understand."

Robbie's face turned slowly scarlet. He considered the worst words he knew in Charlie's vocabulary. "You go to —to Glory," he said and left her.

Belinda considered herself deeply affronted by Robbie's suggestion. But for some time there occurred no opportunity actively to resist it. Correspondence school began, and they did not go into town again for some weeks.

Every morning when breakfast was over, their books
and pencils came out of the dresser drawer and Mrs. Barker
swept the crockery from one end of the kitchen table.
After she had wiped the milk and toast crumbs off of it,
they settled down to their morning's work while she turned
her attention to the washing-up in the sink. Often they
were able to work in silence, but sometimes one would ask
a question, and Mrs. Barker would dry her hands, come
and look over their shoulders, explain the sum, the sen-
tence, or the question, and then return to the washing-up.
Sometimes, glancing over her shoulder, she would see Robbie gazing out of the window at a passing mob of sheep or
Belinda leaning over to snatch his eraser. Then order would
have to be restored before work was resumed.

At other times, while she peeled the vegetables or beat
up a cake, she would have a book open in front of her and
with floury or vegetably hands would turn the pages as she
gave them dictation or asked them lists of spelling. But
there were times, gradually becoming less as they grew up,
when they required her whole attention, and then she
would wash her hands and with unquenchable optimism
pick up her darning basket and sit with it on her lap while
she read or explained or demonstrated. And the morning
would wear on, and from time to time she would look at
the clock until the glorious moment when she said, "All
right, you can go now." And they would sweep their books
into the drawer and rush outside, leaving her to get the
family's dinner in the shortest possible time so that it would
be ready when the men knocked off at midday.

When it was necessary, they worked in the afternoon as
well. It depended on how their quota for the week was
going. Fanny, too young for school, would often remain,

an unquiet ghost in the background; she yearned for the day when she would be allowed to join in the lessons. But sometimes she would play just outside the door, within full view of the workers, and often, infuriatingly, with their belongings, so that school would be disrupted for a time and Mrs. Barker's hair would stand out even more wildly around her forehead.

Perhaps the only person who did not consider Mrs. Barker overworked was Mrs. Barker herself. She thought that no housewife whose home was connected with the main electricity had any reason to grumble at all. She could remember the days of the little electric-light plant that was not strong enough for anything but lights that were never sufficiently bright, and this probably explained why she had had to take to reading glasses at such an early age. She had always thought herself lucky that she did not have to battle with oil lamps, and the day they bought the kerosene refrigerator, after many summers of salted meat, liquid butter, and boiled milk, she had felt that no greater blessing could ever come her way. But now the arrival of main power had brought her the electric iron, the washing machine, and a refrigerator that could be relied on to set a cold pudding even in the hottest weather, and so she felt that all her worries were over. Only the children missed, without even realizing it, the everlasting putt-putt-putt of the little plant in the shed at the back of the house. Somehow for them this had been the sound of home.

One morning, toward the end of breakfast, which they usually had in the kitchen to save time, Mr. Barker suddenly put down his cup, swished the table napkin across the ends of his mustache, and went over to the big wool-firm calendar that hung on the wall. He ran his finger down a column of dates, left it pressed on one square, and turned around.

"Time you went in to Doctor Roberts for your checkup, Ethel," he said accusingly.

"Oh, dear," she said. "But I really haven't time just now, dear."

"Nonsense," he said bracingly. "You know you can always make time, if you try. Organize your days better!"

Mrs. Barker looked at him as if he had suddenly gone demented. Then her face relaxed and she smiled. "Yes, dear," she said meekly.

Jack said more quietly, "You really must go, Mum. The kids can look after their own school for once. When can you go?" he persisted. "This afternoon?"

"Yes," said Mrs. Barker, resigning herself to the inevitable. "I suppose I could. We won't be doing correspondence after lunch, anyway. Are you going in?"

Jack shook his head. "I can't. But I'll fill up the car with gas and bring it around to the front for you."

"I'd much rather wait until you or Dad were going in. You know I hate driving." But this plea had no effect, and in the end she had to go, and Belinda went with her.

All morning, while Belinda should have been thinking of capital cities and the dates of kings, the thought of the Meccano box burned in her brain. She was sure that taking the money would be dishonest, and yet it might be her only chance. It wasn't as if the money was for herself. She was still undecided and feeling rather miserable by the time she went to change. She was up to her hair brushing when the bedroom door was pushed open, and Robbie came in. He walked over to the dressing table that Lorna and Belinda shared and dropped a pile of small change under her nose.

"There," he said gruffly. "You didn't steal it; I did."

So the decision was made for her, and Mrs. Barker found her a helpful and encouraging companion on the drive in, never suspecting that she boiled with so portentous a secret.

Her opportunity for visiting the shop came when Mrs. Barker went up to the doctor's office. Belinda said she would rather wait near where they had parked the car so that she could look in the shop windows. As soon as her mother was out of sight, she darted into the store. It did not take her long to choose what she wanted, but she found that it was necessary to be satisfied with the very cheapest of everything, for the entire contents of the Meccano box was only just enough.

She knew that it would be impossible to keep her knitting a secret from Mrs. Barker, so on the way home she decided that she was now so steeped in guilt that another little white lie would be permissible, and she told her mother that she had been given some knitting to do for Sadie. And she made a mental note of the fact that she must tell Sadie as soon as possible in case her mother happened to mention it.

But her mother was more concerned with the problem of how best to avoid telling her father and Jack that Doctor Roberts was pressing her to make arrangements to go away, and she only half heard what Belinda was saying.

5: The Miner's Tunnel

Of the other three at this stage, Robbie was probably the
only one who was giving their problem much thought.
Both Lorna and Edward were far too busy adjusting themselves to the completely different world of boarding
school.

Robbie, on the contrary, with the tantalizing example of
Belinda coining money with every stitch she made, or so
they both fancied, was always on the lookout for a way to
turn an honest penny. When all's said and done, there are
not many ways for a person of nine to make money. The
scheme to shoot dingoes had fallen through because Mr.
Barker's guns and rifles were not available to persons under
seventeen. Another problem that would have presented
itself if the first had been overcome was that the nearest

dingo country was probably some hundred miles farther west. He had very quickly dismissed the idea of catching rabbits. There was money to be had for skins, but he had been out with Charlie often enough to know what a lot of hard work it involved. He was not strong enough to work the spring traps that Charlie used, and he disliked them anyway.

But one day when he was riding along the riverbank with Jack, he saw a large hole in the side of the bank. He had seen it often enough before and had previously decided that as it was far too big for a rabbit hole, and even too big for a fox, it must have been made by a bear. And he called it in his mind the bear hole. Now it occurred to him that he had never heard of any bears in the district, and he was almost sure there never had been any. Any of the other children could have told him there were no bears except koalas in the whole of Australia, but he had not thought to ask.

"What's that hole for?" he asked as his pony sidled away from it.

"It's an old mine shaft," said Jack, who was watching a cow that he fancied was in the wrong paddock.

"What's that?" asked Robbie.

"A place where they dig metals out of the ground." Jack's mind was, with his eyes, on the cow.

"What metals?"

"Any sort of metals: iron, copper, uranium."

"What did they dig out of this one?"

"Oh, sorry." The beast he had been watching turned out to be in its right place after all, and he turned his full attention to Robbie. "This is only the remains of a shaft where some old fossicker has been looking for gold."

"Gold!" said Robbie, alert at once. "I didn't know there was gold here."

"Well, there isn't," said Jack. "Not enough to get excited about. But there's sometimes a little alluvial gold in the river, and sometimes they find a bit of a vein in the rock. That's what this fellow was looking for."

"Do you reckon he found it?" asked Robbie rather breathlessly.

Jack laughed. "Not likely, or he wouldn't have left it like that. It must be thirty years since that was dug."

"But if he didn't find it, it might be still there, mightn't it?" Dazzling possibilities were unfolding in Robbie's mind that would have astonished Jack if he had guessed.

"It might, but it's very unlikely. There are heaps of those old shafts about in this district, but no one bothers to look for gold any more."

They rode on, and Jack forgot about the conversation. He was more interested in trying to decide whether the amount of dry grass and clover burr there was in the paddocks would hold out until the new growth in the autumn. Of course, if it didn't rain before then, there would be no autumn growth, a state of affairs that Mr. Barker refused to consider, but which Jack, with less optimism but more prudence than his father, kept in the back of his mind as a rather dreadful possibility that might have to be dealt with.

But Robbie did not forget, for he suddenly felt that his opportunity might have arrived. He had almost opened his mouth to tell Jack that he thought of pursuing investigations in the shaft where the fossicker had left off when he remembered that Jack would be almost certain to think of some reason why he shouldn't.

His opportunity to return to the shaft did not occur for some days. But there came an afternoon when Mrs. Barker let them off from their lessons because Mr. Barker had said at dinnertime that he would want them on their ponies afterwards. And when they had presented themselves mounted and ready at the woolshed, they found that things weren't as far ahead as Mr. Barker had thought, and the sheep that were to have gone back to their paddock that afternoon would not be finished till the next day.

Belinda rather crossly unsaddled again, turned her pony loose, and announced that she was going back to her knitting. Robbie watched her go, marveling that anyone should want to give up a heaven-sent free afternoon to knitting and wishing that Edward had not gone off to school.

Thinking of Edward brought his mind back to the task that they had set themselves and that, in turn, switched it to the mine shaft by the river. This looked like his opportunity. Knitting indeed!

He was not quite sure what tools would be best. A pick, he felt, was the proper implement for a job of that sort; yet the shaft, when he thought of it, did not lend itself to pick swinging. In the end he collected a shovel, a crowbar, a trap setter, and a hurricane lamp and with some difficulty attached them, all but the crowbar, to his saddle. The crowbar beat him, and in the end he set forth dragging it behind him, to the astonishment of his long-suffering pony.

It took him quite a time to reach the shaft, for he dropped the heavy crowbar more than once on the way. His arm was very tired by the time he finally let it go on the sand by the river. He flung the pony's rein over the dead root of a tree that had once been swept over by a flood and now lay across the little stretch of sand, a prostrate and rotting giant, with its base and all its roots indecently exposed to the sky. Then he untied his other tools, fished a box of matches out of his pocket, and lit the lamp. Fortunately, there was kerosene in it, for he had not thought to fill it before he left. Then he climbed up the little slope to the shaft. The entrance was almost filled with nettles and tufts of river grass, but he could see the three short, thick beams of wood that outlined the opening. He set to work knocking back the nettles and was smarting in several places before he had finished.

Eventually, he decided the hole was clear enough and squatted down to peer in. It was quite black, and he could see nothing. He reached for the lamp and pushed it in. Its yellow glimmer revealed an opening a good deal smaller than he had imagined, and there were signs that little bits of earth had fallen down from time to time. But it was quite impossible to see beyond the light, so he lay down on his stomach, pushed the lantern ahead of him, and wriggled his shoulders into the hole. Entering in this manner, he had plenty of room, for the shaft had been built to allow for the easy access of a man's shoulders. He wriggled farther and plunged the lantern farther still into the hole. A cold breath came from somewhere in the blackness, but it was heavy with the smell of earth and mold and decay. He wriggled up to the lantern and put his hand out beyond it. The hole seemed to turn a corner, and the dust beneath his palm was powder dry.

He was beginning to wish he had thought to look for snake tracks in and out of the hole before he entered when he suddenly choked, sneezed, and felt his nostrils full of the smell of kerosene. His eyes began to water. He backed out hurriedly, and the kerosene fumes belched out after him. When he had gotten his breath, he plunged in again, grabbed the lamp and pulled it out.

He sat back on his haunches watching the last oily fumes rise from the lamp as the flame adjusted itself once more to an adequate supply of air. The lamp was obviously not a very good idea, and he wondered what he should do next. He did not feel he would be very successful looking for the gold in the dark. A flashlight would be good, but he did not possess one, and there would be endless questions if he asked to borrow his mother's. Then he thought of the matches in his pocket. He pulled them out, reached behind him for the trap setter, and holding both in his hands in front of him, he dived into the shaft once more, elbowing his way in. When he was in up to the belt, he stopped, put down the trap setter, and with some difficulty struck a match.

In its brief flare he saw that the corner was just ahead of him and that a piece of timber supported the roof just over his head. He felt that he must at all costs reach the corner. Any gold there was would be on the other side of it. His mind raced ahead of his body; already he could see himself riding home, his pockets weighed down with egg-sized nuggets, and he began to wish he had thought to bring a bag to put them in. In his excitement he forgot to look carefully at the wooden support above his head. He did not see that it was old and rotten and no longer strong enough for the job it had so many years ago been put there to do.

He wriggled on in the darkness, for by now the match had burnt his fingers, been dropped in the dust, and gone out. The toes of his boots were still just visible to the light of day when he thrust his hands into the darkness ahead of him to try to locate the corner. His matches were limited, and he did not wish to use them unnecessarily. Directly ahead his hands came against a blank earth wall, but at first they met nothing when he reached around to the right. He stretched a bit farther, and the tip of one finger came in contact with something harder than earth. He felt about carefully. It seemed to be a rock face. There were hard lumps on its surface, too. His breath came more quickly, and in something of a frenzy he reached for the matches again. With difficulty he struck one, and laying his cheek on his arm just below the shoulder, he held the flaming match high. There was a patch of rock here that jutted out from the surrounding red earth; some of it was white, like crystal, and some of it glittered. But beyond it the tunnel had either stopped or fallen in; to go any farther, if he wanted to follow the side of rock where it vanished into the earth, he would have to dig.

At this point the match went out. But he thought that he had seen enough. The glittering piece of quartz was still pictured in his memory, and his imagination was enlarging it just a trifle with yellow flecks. He reached underneath him for the trap setter and dragged it forward. He did not think he would be able to keep a match alight while he used it. So, with his cheek still resting on his arm, he thrust his left hand forward, felt for the slab of rock, and grasped the trap setter just behind the neck with his right hand. In a very awkward manner he delivered the first blow.

There was a spark as the steel bounced off the rock. He saw a little scrabble of falling earth, and he could smell the dust in his nostrils. He stopped and laboriously struck another match. It flickered dimly in the dust-laden air, but he could see a little pocket where his tool had struck, and before the match went out, he thought he saw a gleam in the piece of rock he had just uncovered. His excitement increased, although he did not realize it, beyond the bounds of safety. Once more he grasped the trap setter, once more he felt for the point to aim at, and this time he put all the force he knew into the blow. The head of the tool bounced against the rock and sprang back. Without taking aim he struck again and again, and the force of his blows jerked and twisted his small body in the hole. It forced his hips in one wild plunge against the piece of rotten timber above him. There was a crack and a thump, and clods of earth began to bump onto the small of his back. At first he was not particularly alarmed. He stopped digging and lay still, and the clods stopped falling; but the air was now very full of dust, and it was getting hard to breathe. Reluctantly, he decided he had better wriggle out.

Before he started, he struck another match but found he could scarcely open his eyes for grit and dust, and the beam of light was not strong enough to penetrate it. He maneuvered the matches back into his pocket, grasped the trap setter, and prepared to move. He could still feel the weight on the small of his back, but it did not seem very heavy. He shifted a fraction of an inch backwards and felt a prick where the weight was. He moved forward and tried again. Again there was the prick, and this time he pushed against it. It became sharper, more painful and did not seem at all inclined to shift. He slid his hand down behind him and felt the earth piled up around his hips. Raising it higher, he discovered the beam of timber, but it no longer supported the roof. His last convulsive blow had snapped it in the middle, and one sharp, broken end now came down at an angle of forty-five degrees and rested, together with the earth it had dislodged, in the middle of his back. Every time he moved it rested a little more firmly, a little more sharply, on his backbone.

In sudden panic he heaved and pushed. The pain was horrible, and the rotten timber squeaked and groaned as it gave way further. More and heavier lumps of earth descended on his back. In sudden terror and with the pain of his back, he screamed and then began to cry. But the scream was deadened and muffled in the little hole, whose supply of air was more and more being cut off, and the effort of crying forced him to swallow the dust. He dared not move, and after a few minutes he was quiet.

And now, when he was forced to stop and think, he began to understand to the full just how grim his situation was, and a cold, deathly terror began to creep over him. He no longer dared move to try to get out. If he did, he might start the earth moving again, and the whole hillside might descend on top of him, and the piece of timber—but at this point he began to whimper softly to himself and his imagination refused to go further. It shied away from the immediate situation and began to wander away and up into the light. Up at the house it must be nearly teatime. Belinda would be putting the fowls to bed; Jack would be coming back from putting up the calves. His mother would probably be bending over the bathtub trying to get the day's grime off Fanny. There would be something on the stove, and its smell would float out of the kitchen door to welcome the returning workers. This unbidden picture only served to sharpen his mental misery until he began to wonder when they would miss him. Then a faint hope stirred.

He knew that his only hope now was that someone should find him and dig him out. There was nothing more he could do for himself. But he was often late for tea. It might be a long time before they would even miss him. His mother, surely his mother would miss him? Surely she would somehow know he needed help? She knew all sorts of funny things. But how would they find him when they didn't even know where he'd gone? He had told no one where he was going, and what would make them think of the river when there were so many other places he might have gotten to?

He felt the sudden, blinding onrush of claustrophobia, a feeling that, though it killed him, he must get out, and his muscles tensed for the final frenzied effort that would have brought the tunnel down on top of him. But he never made it. An effort of will that nearly cracked his sinews stopped him in the nick of time. It saved his life and brought out a quality of character that afterwards, as he grew older, was never to leave him. Then he lay quiet.

Outside the shaft the still, warm summer evening began to draw in. Insects darted and floated over the quiet, wide reaches of the river, and sometimes the surface was ruffled by the stealthy movements of a water rat. In the branches of the casuarinas the magpies gurgled their last song. Here and there a swallow darted after its evening meal or flickered over the river leaving a little circle of disturbed water where its beak had touched. The sun sank below the rolling line of hilltops, and shadows gathered under the trees. The pony stamped and moved and began to grow restless, and the lantern still burned where Robbie had left it, for he had forgotten to blow it out.

Then a small branch from somewhere high up in the tree

above broke loose and came rustling and crackling its
way down. It fell with a little crash not far from the pony's
nose, and he jumped back, for he was prepared and almost
eager to be frightened by something. He strained at the
reins, and one of his hind hoofs hit the lantern. It fell over
on its side, and there was a little tinkle as the glass broke.
The pony stood still, straining to the full extent of his
reins, with his nose stretched out. The lantern flame, which
had almost gone out when it fell over, slowly gathered
strength as the wick found a little pool of kerosene and
gratefully soaked it up. Just above the lantern one of the
branches of the dead tree to which the pony was tied dan-
gled its tufts of dead, dry needles. And now the little
flame gathered strength and lengthened until, reaching up
as if it were hungry, it caught the tips of the pine needles.
There was a sudden swish, a roar, and a crackling, and the
oncoming night was halted by the blossoming fire. The
pony heard the noise, saw the blaze of light, and felt the
sudden heat behind him. It was too much, and with one
desperate wrench he sat on his haunches and jerked his
head backwards. The reins gave way with a snap, and he
whirled on his hocks and raced for home.

The fire, once under way and generating heat, began to
blaze merrily. There were plenty of dry leaves, dead sticks,
and bits of flotsam thrown up by the river for fuel, and
there was not an atom of moisture in any of it.

Up at the house they did not notice the fire immediately,
for the shoulder of a nearby hill hid the riverbank from
view. But Mrs. Barker, from force of habit, always began
counting heads when she started to lay the table. And now,
not being able to get a proper tally no matter which end
she started, she put the bread board down on the dining-

room table and called to Jack, who was taking his boots off on the edge of the veranda, "Where did Robbie go? Do you know?"

"No," called Jack over his shoulder. "Can't say I noticed, Mum. Ask Belinda; she was with him."

But all Belinda knew was that he had gone off somewhere on his pony.

"Well, have a look around, Jack, will you?" said Mrs. Barker. "He may be hanging around the sheds somewhere, and we can't wait tea. Your father's hungry."

Patiently, Jack pulled on his boots again and climbed to his feet. Afterwards he was glad that he had.

Robbie was nowhere to be seen at the woolshed, at the kennels, at the fowl house, and Jack was trudging, rather irritated, back to the house to tell his mother it was no use waiting when he heard a horse's whinny and the thump of hooves. He looked up expecting to find Robbie returning and saw, indeed, the pony's head and shoulders approaching at speed over the brow of the nearest hill. But something about the pony attracted his further attention, and he looked more carefully. Then he noticed that the reins were swinging loose and the pony kept jerking his nose in the air to avoid treading on them. Alarmed now, he turned and walked toward him and saw as the pony cantered toward him that the saddle was empty.

He caught him as the pony came up to him, gathered the broken ends of the reins, and sprang into the saddle, folding the short stirrups across the pommel. Then he turned and cantered quickly in the direction the pony had come from.

Once over the hill he saw the smoke, a black, angry column rising from the river, and saw the red glow at the heart of it. He turned and made the surprised pony gallop back toward the house. At the back garden gate he shouted for his father without bothering to get off. When the round red face with its startled white whiskers appeared around the kitchen door, he said hurriedly, "There's a fire started down at the river just beyond the bend. Stir up Charlie and bring the fire cart. I'm going straight down. I think Robbie may be in a bit of bother down there. Don't tell Mum, but better get her to tell the Trevors and the other neighbors about the fire. It may not be much, but you can't tell." He swung the pony around and went off before Mr. Barker had time to reply.

Fortunately, there was no wind, and the fire had not spread any distance. The dead tree was alight for its whole length, and a live tree near it had caught and reared like a great torch into the violet sky, sending blazing twigs and leaves splashing and hissing into the water below. Some of the tussocky river grass had caught and was burnt, but fortunately the fire had not yet crept up over the lip of the bank into the grassy slopes of the hills. Peering down from the top of the bank, Jack could make out the black length of the crowbar, though it took him a few seconds to realize what it was. The sight of it, however, was enough to tell him that this was where Robbie had been. He took the pony a little way to windward of the fire, tied it securely, and hoped it would remain there. Then he made his way down to the river on foot and turned toward the fire.

It grew very hot as he approached, and he had to shield his face with his hand. As he walked, he searched the ground and glanced occasionally toward the dark lip of the river. But he saw nothing, and as he approached the fire, his steps became more urgent.

He stopped some yards from the dead tree because it was almost impossible to get closer. But all around him the ground was illuminated as clearly as by daylight. He saw the marks in the sand where the pony had been standing. And then, blackened now and almost unrecognizable, he saw the upturned lantern. The broken glass, glinting in the

firelight, showed him where it was. At any rate, he knew
now how the fire had started. But there was no sign at all
of Robbie.

He walked down to the water's edge, climbing and slipping over the round gray boulders, until he could look up-
stream and downstream across the black water. It told him
nothing, and he had, in any case, little fear that Robbie
might have drowned, for he was a safe, if unconventional,
swimmer. He went up toward the bank, being deceived
from time to time by the moving shadows flung by the
fire into thinking he saw a body lying there. But there was
no body. And he was considering whether he should cast
his search wider when another burst of flame high in the
standing casuarina lit up the old mine shaft. With his hands
protecting his face, he stepped toward it. He could not
have said why, except that without actually thinking
about it, he sensed a connection between the mine shaft and
the broken lantern. As soon as he came close to it, he noticed the broken and scattered nettles, the tufts of grass
wrenched out; and now, looking down at his feet by the
entrance of the shaft, he could see the trampled, recently
disturbed earth.

He dropped quickly to his hands and knees. He knew the
dangers of these old shafts, and he cursed himself for not
warning Robbie when they passed by the other day, for he
remembered now that Robbie had asked about it.

The side of him that faced the fire was almost hotter
than he could bear, but he clenched his teeth and did his
best to ignore it. He looked carefully at the entrance of the
hole, saw in the flickering light that the entrance was partially blocked by loose earth, and began scraping the earth
toward him. His breath came more quickly, but it was

neither with exertion nor heat. He had scooped perhaps two handfuls when his hands fell on something hard. Thinking it a stone, he tried to drag it out with the earth, but it would not come. He felt more carefully and discovered there were two of—whatever it was. Quickly he scraped more earth away and felt again. This time he was sure. They were Robbie's shoes, and with a sort of groan he began to dig feverishly. The legs of his trousers were beginning to singe, but he did not notice it. It was not difficult to uncover the thin, bony ankles, and he found with some relief that he was breaking through the heap of earth in the entrance, and the legs up to just above the knee were free. But they were very still, and when he squeezed them, there was no responding movement.

He could see no farther into the shaft, but his hands told him that beyond the knees the shaft had fallen in again. He started to dig in reckless haste and then stopped. He thought for a minute and then backed out quickly and picked up the crowbar. It was hot to the touch, but he spat on his palms before taking it to the shaft. He pushed it in slowly, guiding the point with his hand. Bit by bit it went into the earth over the motionless body. When it stuck, he twisted and worked and edged it forward, being careful now not to make any sudden movement. After probably about five minutes of this patient manipulation, the point of the bar ran up against something firm and solid. He guessed that he had met rock and could go no farther, and he had, in fact, come up against the face where the shaft turned. The point of the bar was now rather higher than the base and slowly, resting the bar on his shoulder, he lifted it.

It was pure chance that made him put the bar just under

the broken beam, and as he raised it, the murderous point began to lift little by little off Robbie's backbone. At the corner the beam still held, so that as it came up, it gave more support to what was left of the roof. When the bar was level, Jack began to dig again. Carefully and quickly, with the bar still resting on his shoulders, he scooped the fallen earth down toward the entrance of the hole. Feeling with his hands as he dug, he discovered the broken beam and understood, then, exactly what had happened. To his relief, at about Robbie's shoulder blades the shaft became clear again. He wriggled himself farther in, pressing the bar against the roof with his back, and felt along Robbie's body with his hands. He found the shoulders, the arms stretched out in front, the neck, and the small dust-covered head. But he could feel no movement.

There was no time to find out if Robbie still breathed, but having made sure that the whole body was now clear, Jack began to ease it backwards. It was difficult, because he was forced to support the roof at the same time. But at last, with a gasp of relief, he got Robbie clear of the hole, drew his head out, and took a great breath of air; and although it was warm and full of the tang of smoke, it seemed marvelously fresh to him.

Quickly he bent down, picked up the light body, and carried it away from the fire. He laid it down on the first flat piece of ground and put his face to Robbie's mouth. For a moment he thought he could detect nothing. Then, as he ceased to breathe himself, he felt, or thought he felt, the tiniest flutter of breath between the lips. He put his head closer and shut his eyes. It came again, and there was no mistaking it this time. He snatched up the grimy hand and felt for the pulse. It was beating, too, lightly but unmistakably. He took a huge breath, picked Robbie up again, and headed for home.

As he expected, he met the fire cart before he had gone very far. He told his father quickly what had happened, cutting short exclamations that threatened to be more than usually dramatic by saying that he thought Robbie would be all right if he could get him home quickly, and would they get the water tank off the truck so that he could drive it back. This was not easy, but the sight of Robbie, limp and still in his arms, encouraged them to superhuman efforts, and somehow, emptying out a great deal of the water, they got it off. While they threw out the rakes and leather beaters, Jack put Robbie gently on the seat and got in himself.

"See to the pony, will you?" he shouted as he put his foot on the starter. The last rake came out as the truck moved forward.

Five minutes later, as he carried Robbie into the kitchen, he said quickly, "He'll be all right, Mum."

And in a couple of hours he was, if not quite back to normal, at least "all right." Bit by bit his breathing grew stronger and the blue look left his face and lips, and by the time Doctor Roberts arrived, his eyelids were beginning to flutter.

Doctor Roberts whistled when Jack told him where Robbie had been found, said he was very lucky to be alive, and started to inspect him for further damage. Mrs. Barker clapped her hand over her mouth when they rolled him over on his face, and she saw where the red stain had soaked through his shirt in the small of his back. But after all it was only a small gash, and at the time not even Jack could think how it got there.

Before Doctor Roberts left, with instructions that he should spend the next day in bed, Robbie's eyes were properly open, and he demanded food and drink. By bedtime he appeared to be his normal self, and they would have thought him quite recovered if, much later that night and for several subsequent nights, he had not awakened them all with a succession of nightmares.

The fire, fortunately, had never gotten completely out of control, and although they kept a careful watch on it for a couple of days afterwards, it did little damage beyond making a blackened ghost of one tree and singeing several others. It was fortunate that at that time there was no wind at all.

Because of the nightmares Mrs. Barker would not let Robbie's father utter the terse and telling words he wished to. The nightmares, she said, were punishment and reminder enough. Robbie himself told them little of his adventure, for he had no wish to be reminded of it. But he lost all interest in gold mining and from that day decided to make what money he could by the safe, if laborious, method of catching rabbits.

Jack was let off the milking for several days because of his blistered hands, and Mrs. Barker reluctantly decided that his trousers had been too badly singed to repair. Once she said to Robbie when they were alone, "You must always be grateful to Jack because he saved your life, you know, and got quite badly burnt doing it." Robbie had said nothing, only nodded, and his eyes had grown so big and dark that she put her arm around his shoulders and squeezed them quickly, an unusually demonstrative action for her.

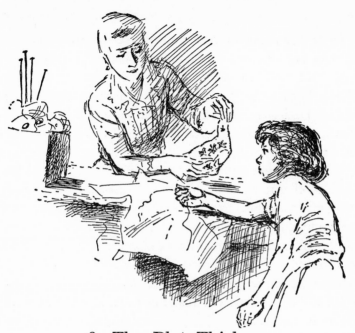

6: The Plot Thickens

For Belinda, too, all was not plain sailing, although her lesson was not as sharp and dramatic as Robbie's. She finished the jacket not long after he had had his accident and then proceeded to embroider it lavishly, mainly over her mistakes. The colors that she chose were what she would have described as cheerful, and when she had finished, the jacket looked, if a little uneven, at least extremely gay.

When the next opportunity offered, she took it with her to Bungaree. Finding an excuse to slip off by herself, she went a little nervously into the baby shop. The lady was busy at the shelves when she entered but, hearing her, turned and came over to the counter.

"Yes, dear?" she said with a faintly exotic accent. "What would you like?"

Belinda swallowed and pushed the parcel onto the counter in front of her. "I thought you might like to— to buy this for your shop."

The lady, looking surprised, took it and unfolded the paper. To Belinda, the little jacket thus revealed looked worse than she remembered it. It was forcibly impressed on her at that moment that it is one thing to make garments for the tolerant eyes of one's family and friends and quite another to make them with the intention of changing them into something as uncompromising as money. All her little mistakes, which her mother would tactfully have ignored, seemed to shout of their existence.

The lady said nothing for a minute or so but looked carefully at the garment, turned it over, and finally held it up in front of her. Belinda felt that this minute inspection was somehow unfair.

"You say you wish to sell this to me?"

Belinda swallowed and nodded.

"You have worked hard at this, yes? All these flowers are a lot of work."

Again Belinda nodded, her face an extremely interesting shade of deep brick. Then the lady said, "Wait. I show you," and plucked something off the shelf behind her. She spread it on the counter; a jacket very similar to Belinda's but with only one very small embellishment, and that in white. But there was not one mistake in it. The lady let her look at it before she spoke and then said, "A lot of people are very, very fussy about mistakes. They can make them with mistakes themselves, but the ones with no mistakes in them, those are the ones they buy." Then she picked up Belinda's again. "But myself, I think yours is very pretty. I like these bright colors, and I should like to buy this one from you for myself. Shall I give you five shillings for it?"

Belinda's woebegone mouth suddenly split into a brilliant smile, and she said, "Oh yes, please. That would be lovely, thank you, if you don't think five shillings is too much."

The lady smiled at this unbusinesslike approach and shook her head. "I take it, then," she said and whisked it away, placing five shillings on the counter in front of Belinda. Then she leaned forward, her arms on the counter.

"If you want to make things for me," she said, "there is more money for sewing, and I need plenty of little nightgowns. But"—she smiled quickly—"they must be good. No mistakes and no big stitches. Look, I give you one to take." She went to the back of the shop and came back with a baby's nightdress, which she laid on the counter. "This one," she said, "I cannot sell because I singed it with the iron." She indicated a brownish patch on the skirt. "But if you like, you may take it and copy it. You would like to?"

Belinda nodded, almost beyond speech. "If I make some just like this," she said at last, "will you buy them?"

"Yes," said the lady. "If they are just like that and most carefully made, I will buy them from you for a pound each."

Belinda took the five shillings and bought herself as much of the best material as she could afford at the general store. She found it necessary to ask her mother how much she needed, and her mother showed some surprise at her sudden ardor for making baby clothes.

"Surely Sadie doesn't want all these?" she said.

Belinda decided that partial honesty would be the best course. "Oh no, this isn't for Sadie. This is for the lady at the baby shop. She's going to give me a whole pound if I make it nicely."

"Goodness gracious!" said Mrs. Barker. "If she's going to give you all that, you'll have to make it very carefully indeed." And after that she watched Belinda's sewing closely and helped her when she thought it necessary because, as she explained, "If you are to get all that money for it, you must be sure it's your very best work—otherwise it wouldn't be honest."

With Robbie now committed to the undramatic, slow, but ultimately rewarding task of catching rabbits, and Belinda with her promised market for good and careful sewing, the home team was keeping its end up well, and if the money-making efforts were neither as swift nor as entertaining as they had imagined, this in itself was a valuable lesson well learned.

The boarding school pair, on the other hand, were greatly handicapped by their surroundings. Lorna, having settled down to the new term, began to think again of what her contribution could be. She had heard from her mother of Robbie's adventure and knew quite well, though her mother did not, what had impelled him to go seeking gold with such reckless impetuosity. Secretly, she felt proud of him. She wrote him a letter, telling him how glad she was that he was safe and sound again. She dared not say too much, for she suspected that her mother might see the letter. Then she began to think hard.

She had been thinking for three weeks and was nearly in despair when her friend, Penny Andrews, said something that gave her the beginnings of an idea.

They were reading their letters, which had just arrived, when Penny looked up and said, "Oh, poor Jill. She is having stinking luck."

"Why?" asked Lorna, who knew that Jill was Penny's married sister who lived in Sydney.

"That's the third horrid girl who's walked out on her."

"Oh," said Lorna. "What a shame! Why has this one gone?"

"The same old story," said Penny gloomily. "Two small children and a baby are too much to manage." She stopped and thought for a while, her chin in her palm, and then said, "Lorna, are children so terribly hard to look after?"

"No, of course not," said Lorna, who regarded the minding of three or more small children as just part of ordinary life. "I suppose they just don't know how."

"I suppose so," said Penny. "And it's not as if Jill ever expects them to do much—just feed the kids in the middle of the day and take them for a walk or something in the afternoon. You'd think it would be easy, wouldn't you?"

"It *would* be easy," said Lorna positively.

"I suppose if Jill can't find anyone to do it, she'll have to give up her music. It is a shame. It isn't as if she doesn't pay them enough, either. *Pounds* a week. She told me once and said if it wasn't that she felt she was doing more good keeping on with her music, she'd easily do it herself. It would be cheaper, she said."

Lorna could not help remembering Penny's casual phrase, "pounds a week," and the conclusion she came to was that so much money merely for minding children could only be gross overpayment. A further thought told her that if money was to be made by doing something as simple as that, she might as well be the one to make it.

At first she said nothing to Penny, but she continued to think about it. There were difficulties, and the worst of them was that she could hardly be looking after someone's children and attending boarding school at the same time. She knew quite well which she would rather do but doubted if even her father, who was far less conscientious about school than her mother, would agree with her.

Then one day when they were discussing the holidays, Penny asked Lorna what she was going to do.

"Go home, I suppose, like I always do," said Lorna, slightly surprised that Penny should think she might be doing anything else.

"Well, you're lucky," said Penny. "I bet I have to go and stay with Jill and help her with the kids."

"Wouldn't you like to?" asked Lorna.

"No fear," said Penny. "I'm not used to young brothers and sisters like you. I'd rather be at home and go out with Mum and things. Of course," she added pensively, "Jill always gives me something when I go and help, and that wouldn't be bad."

It was when another letter came from Jill, saying that she hadn't been able to find anyone at all and would just have to rely on Penny's help in the holidays, that Lorna took the plunge and said, "Penny, suppose I spent the holidays with her? I'm sure I could manage."

Penny's mouth dropped open. "But don't you want to go home? You're so mad about your home and your sisters and brothers and everything."

"I know," Lorna said with a sudden sinking feeling. "But I've just *got* to earn some money. And I don't know how else to do it."

Penny looked so astonished at this that Lorna felt obliged to tell her the whole story. She swore her to secrecy, and Penny listened in awestruck silence until the end. Then she put both hands on Lorna's arm and said, "Lorna, I've got some money in the savings bank; my godmother put it there for me. I'll *give* it to you. Mum's always telling me to be generous, and this is a bit of generous I would enjoy being."

Lorna turned to her with gratitude. "Oh, Penny, you are kind. But I couldn't possibly just *take* money." Considering she had been prepared to do anything to get it, she did not quite know why she said this, but without trying to work it out, she knew that it was so, and to take money from Penny was quite out of the question. Instead, she said, "But if you could, perhaps, ask your sister, Jill—?"

"I will. I'll write to her this very day. I'll leave my Latin homework till the morning. And I'll tell Jill how good you are with children. She'll be thrilled. And she'll think I'm so clever to have found someone for her."

"Do you—do you think she would mind paying me?" asked Lorna with some embarrassment.

"Of course not," said Penny. "Especially when I tell her what experience you've had. That's a thing they always ask, I know."

"I think," said Lorna, "it would be best if you just said I'm used to children. I wouldn't like her to think I was so wonderful and then find I wasn't."

"Leave it to me," said Penny. "I won't tell her a thing. I do think it's a wonderful idea. And another heavenly thing is that I'll be able to see you in the holidays."

To Lorna, who was beginning to have misgivings, it did not seem long before Penny came to say that it was all fixed up. Jill would like to see Lorna one day when it could be arranged.

"So next time I go home on a Sunday," said Penny, "you must come with me and have an interview."

From then until she had her interview, Lorna wished with all her heart that she had never thought of it. She had never before stayed in anyone's home but her own, she had practically never been in the city in her life, except in the few comings and goings to school, and, worst of all, she had never wanted so much to go home as she did these next holidays. If it had not been for the amount of money she would be able to earn and the great need there was for it, she could not have borne the idea for a moment. But she did not mention this to Penny, for it seemed to her rude and ungrateful.

After the interview it was better. Jill was an easy, friendly person who seemed delighted at the thought of having Lorna for the holidays, and insisted on paying her what Lorna thought a far too princely sum. But she did ask one difficult question.

"Do your parents know you are coming to me? And are they willing to spare you for the holidays?"

To this Lorna had to reply "yes," though she knew quite well that it was not true. And it was lucky for her that Jill did not find time to carry out her original intention of writing at once to Mrs. Barker.

Feeling the need to confess to someone, Lorna wrote to Edward. She received the following letter:

Dear Lorna, Thanks for your letter. It was almost as good as getting one from home. You've got all the luck. There's no way I can see to make money hear. I got to think hard but reckon I'll have to leave it to the holidays now. I wish they'd hurry. It seems years since I came and

*don't tell Mum but I don't like it too well. The boys hear
are a funny lot 'cept one or two that come from the bush
somewhere. I don't seem to learn their names too well or
understand what their talking about harf the time. Everyone's in such a terrible hurry all the time I can't seem to
see why yet. But I'll get used to it I suppose. Your loving
brother Edward. P.S. Did Mum tell you about Robbie?
They haven't forgotten, then. But hope him and Linda
don't kill themselves getting it.*

About the same time Edward wrote to his mother:

*Dear Mum, Thanks for your letter. You don't have to
worry about me. Everything's fine hear and getting on
well. We play cricket in the afternoon if you can play that
is. Yes the food's all right, at least I can swallow it. Some of
the boys say they can't. Yes of course their nise boys. Yes
I got some friends. Yes I'm well at least just ordinary so I
suppose that's well. Mum are you well you didn't say so I
hope so. Sorry about Robbie getting stuck in the hole. He
ort to have more sense but glad Jack got him out all right.
Your loving son Edward. P.S. Only seven weeks three
days four hours and fifty-two minutes till we go home.*

He also wrote to Robbie:

*Dear Rob, I hope you are well. Sorry to hear you got
stuck in the hole. Was pleased you haven't forgotten but
you don't have to try that hard. You'll end up being more
trouble than help but glad you got out. Good old Jack.
School's all right but no good for young kids. You
wouldn't like it. We play cricket and things like that. You*

*need to have your muscle up. Your loving brother Ed-
ward. P.S. Good on you though for trying.*

The effect of this letter on Robbie was to stir him from
his disheartened and still rather dazed inactivity and send
him up to the rabbit pack kennels one evening to see Charlie.

Charlie had just pegged out his rabbit skins and was
throwing the carcases to the dogs.

"Hullo, mate," he said as Robbie approached. "They tell
me you been trying to get rich quick." His dirty, hairy old
face creased in appreciation of his own wit, and his shoulders shook.

Robbie was not amused. He wished, in fact, that the
story had not gotten about the station; but he wanted information from Charlie, so he swallowed his annoyance and
said, "That's right, Charlie." And he forced an unconvinc-
ing smile. Then, before Charlie could think up any more
similar witticisms, he said, "How can I catch rabbits, Charlie?"

"How can you catch rabbits, eh?" said Charlie, whose
habit it was to repeat all questions put to him, particularly
those of children, in the manner of a music-hall stooge.

"Yes," said Robbie patiently and hoped that for once
Charlie would take him seriously. "I want to catch some
rabbits, and I can't open those iron traps like you use."

"Well now," said Charlie portentously, and his faded blue
eyes twinkled. "O' course you could foller the rabbit down
the hole like you done before, couldn't you? Or you could
stalk 'im with your little catapult. And then again you
could kinda pounce on 'im when he's asleep under a tus-
sock—" He paused and waited for an appreciative word

from his audience. It was not forthcoming, so he went on, "Or then again you could make one o' those wire nettin' funnel traps and poke it down the hole."

Robbie recognized this as the real thing at last and hastened to drop in an encouraging word. "Yes, I could. How would I make it?"

Charlie scratched his head. "I dunno can I tell you how. Look, you run over to the shed where me tucker box is, and you'll see a bit of a length of nettin' lying about. Bring it here and I'll show yer."

Robbie raced off, hoping that Charlie's helpful mood would survive the delay. He found the length with no trouble and returned with it quickly. Charlie took the netting, spread it out, rolled it, turned it, twisted it, all the time to the accompaniment of stertorous breathing, and finally fastened the last little threads of wire down and handed it to Robbie. It was now a cone-shaped funnel, closed at the wide end and open at the narrow with a wire-netting door, swinging from a hinge above, a few inches in from the narrow opening that could be pushed open inward but not out.

"See that?" he said. "All you do is find a burrer the rabbits are using, block up all the holes but one, and poke this down."

"And will the rabbits go into this?" Robbie asked.

"Should do," said Charlie. "You try and see."

So Robbie went off with the trap to a private burrow that he knew of and poked it down as Charlie had told him. The following morning he slipped out just before school to see what the night had brought and, to his joy, saw that the trap contained a rabbit. He extracted it, killed it in the quick and painless manner that Jack had taught him, and reset the trap. Then he returned to the house and started

his lessons. During school, when he should have been mem-
orizing tables, it occurred to him that the more traps he
had, the more rabbits he would catch.

From then on he began to make progress. There were
lots of little pieces of wire netting lying about, as there always are around the working part of a property, and several of them were big enough for his traps. The first one
looked rather strange when he had finished it, so he waited
for Charlie's return at the end of the day and had it put
right. After that he put three or four quite creditable traps
together on his own. Then he set about finding holes to put
them in, and this took a little time, for a lot of the once
likely holes had been dug out by Charlie. However, eventually he had them all placed, and thereafter every day,
either early or late, he patrolled his trap line. It was ener-
getic work, for he found that it was not practicable to take
the pony. Some of the best burrows were on steep hillsides or among rocks where the pony could not go, and on
his own he could ignore the gates and cut straight across
country, thereby halving the time it took him to go
around them. He found on an average about one rabbit a
day. Sometimes there were none, and he walked his trap
line for nothing, and sometimes there were two, or even
three, and by the time he reached the house with them he
began to wonder if it were sheep and not rabbits he was
carrying on his back.

Having gotten them home, he had to skin them, and although he knew well enough how to do it, for Jack had
shown him several times, it was a laborious business with
the first half a dozen. After that he began to get quicker.
He stretched each skin on a piece of bent fencing wire and
hung it on a beam in the woolshed out of the reach of cats,

dogs, or rats. And little by little the line of skins increased until the sight of them gave him considerable satisfaction.

Jack, unknown to Robbie, had also been watching the line of skins grow and wondered that his youngest brother should display such perseverance, a quality that no one had reason to suspect in him up till now. Not even Robbie could have told him that those terrifying hours in the mine shaft had taught him lessons one is not usually obliged to learn until much later. He did, however, ask Robbie why he was collecting skins and received the inadequate reply that he wanted the money. This was on the day after Robbie, Fanny, and Belinda had been taken into Bungaree for one of the government-sponsored injection campaigns, and Robbie had been forced to speak politely for a few moments to an elderly acquaintance of his mother's. This lady, the wife of a shopkeeper newly arrived from the city, had prised out of him the information that he was collecting rabbit skins and told him then that it was a cruel and wicked occupation and that she was surprised he should be allowed to pursue it. This startled Robbie more than a little, for he had been brought up to think the extermination of rabbits, by any means, one of the cardinal virtues because they were so destructive and so numerous. The next day, as Jack happened to come into the shed when he was stretching his skins, he said, "Do you reckon catching rabbits is wrong, Jack?"

Jack looked at him in some surprise. "I certainly hope not," he said. "Because we've got to do it. Why?"

So Robbie told him about the conversation he'd had in Bungaree.

Jack sat down on a bale of crutchings and crossed one leg over the other. He was not often approached on moral issues, and he had to gather his thoughts. After a few moments while he silently watched another skin being added to the line, he said, "Lots of fellows kill things for sport: duck, hares, pigs, as well as rabbits and dingoes and kangaroos that you've often got to kill anyway; and I don't go much on that myself. I never could see the fun in killing things when you haven't got to. But with rabbits, it's a case of them or us, and if we didn't kill 'em, we'd have to turn the place over to them sooner or later and just leave, and I can't see that anyone would expect us to do that. Even if we did, they'd pretty soon starve themselves out and die anyway. I can't see anything wrong with trying to prevent that, can you?"

Robbie shook his head. Then he looked up and grinned.

"I didn't really think it was wicked," he said. "I just wanted to know what to say next time she starts chewing my ear."

7: Belinda Falls from Grace

Jack might have been suspicious of Robbie's sudden urge to wealth if he had happened to notice that Belinda, too, was displaying more diligence than she usually did, though her efforts were more spasmodic than Robbie's. There were times when she sewed in every spare minute of the day and even in her bed at night, taking care that her mother should not see the light.

Belinda, in fact, was beginning to have some sucesss with her sewing. Having confessed as much as she dared to her mother, she was able to ask her for advice when she needed it, with the result that the first nightgown, when it was completed, looked better than she had dared to hope. It had certainly taken her longer than she had expected, and she began to see that considerable effort would be necessary if she were to show a reasonable profit when Lorna and Edward came home for the holidays. The shop lady's satisfaction and the crisp pound note that Belinda afterwards held in her hand encouraged her to carry on, and she took to sewing in bed more and more, shading the light so that it should not be seen, screwing up her eyes and holding the sewing under her nose in an effort to see sufficiently in the dim light. Ordinarily speaking, she was not noted for her constancy of effort; she was, in fact, rather lazy. But there was a charm in this clandestine way of working that appealed to her, and there were nights when she sewed so long that her eyes began to sting and water and her head to ache. It was quite some time before Mrs. Barker noticed the redness of her eyes in the mornings and longer still before she began to take it seriously. By the time she did, more than one piece of clothing had found its way into the baby shop and several pound notes into the Meccano box, and the May holidays were almost upon them.

One morning Belinda's eyes were so sore that she was not able to do her lessons. She battled on for some time without complaining, for she did not want her mother to know what was wrong. But a pain in the eyes is more depressing than any other sort of pain, and she was struggling to read aloud from a geography book with small print. When Fanny appeared around the corner of the kitchen table wearing one of the half-finished nightgowns on her head and the nightgown looked as if it had been used with some vigor as a duster, Belinda found it more than her strained self-control could stand. Mrs. Barker turned toward her with a half-peeled potato in her hand in time to see Belinda's face turn brick red, her book suddenly fly across the table, and Fanny, propelled by a sharp blow in her small chest from Belinda's elbow, sent spinning across the kitchen to land on her back against the saucepan stand so that every saucepan but one fell with a clatter on top of her. The nightgown had been snatched from her head together with a handful of her hair, and she had every reason to raise the immediate and earsplitting screech that she did. But it was almost too much for normal eardrums, and Mrs. Barker dropped the potato and clapped her hands to her head. Belinda dropped her head on her arms and burst into tears.

Robbie, from his place at the far end of the kitchen table, looked on placidly. He was accustomed to crises; they occurred fairly frequently in the Barker family, and his emotions were merely those of objective interest coupled with

satisfaction that an interruption had taken place in the lesson.

Mrs. Barker went over to Fanny, picked her up, wiped her nose, and put the saucepans back on the stand. Fanny appeared to have sustained no major injury, so she returned to the sink.

"Go outside, please, Fanny," she said calmly. "Leave Belinda's things alone and don't come into the kitchen during lessons. I've told you that before."

Fanny gave her sobbing sister a black and smoldering look and silently took herself off. Mrs. Barker turned her attention to Belinda.

"That'll do now, Belinda," she said not unkindly but a little wearily. "It's not as bad as all that. The nightgown will wash. And another time please don't hit Fanny like that. You might have injured her. Go on with the Eskimos and the North Pole now please." To her surprise this brought a fresh bout of sobs, and Belinda raised a sodden and glistening face.

"I can't," she said. "My eyes hurt."

Once more Mrs. Barker put down the potato. She looked closely at her daughter's face. At this moment it was not a particularly attractive sight, and it seemed not unnatural that her eyes should appear red and puffy.

"Don't be silly, dear," she said. "Blow your nose, wipe your eyes, and try again."

"I can't," wailed Belinda once more. "They've been hurting all morning, and now they're dreadfully sore." She dissolved once more in an ecstasy of sobs.

Robbie now regarded her with mild disgust. "Cut it out," he said. "You're wetting the book, and they'll be angry with us."

But Belinda was past caring. The many nights of sewing when she should have been sleeping had worn her down, and now with the pain in her eyes she had no more fight left in her. Mrs. Barker left the sink and walked around the table. She took Belinda's chin in her hand and looked speculatively into her face.

"Very well," she said at last. "If they're really too sore, you'd better leave the lessons this morning. Go and lie down on your bed and have a rest, and we'll see how they are this afternoon." And to Robbie's annoyance she turned to him. "You carry on with the Eskimos, Robbie," she said and returned to the vegetables in the sink.

By the afternoon it was clear to Mrs. Barker that something would have to be done about Belinda's eyes. She had searched in vain for eyelashes, grains of sand, and tiny insects. Resignedly, she began to plan to take Belinda to the nearest oculist, sixty miles away in Orange.

"Good grief," said Mr. Barker loudly when she told him. "What's come over this family? If Robbie's not getting stuck in rabbit burrows, Belinda's going cross-eyed. Are we never to have any peace again?" He swung around on his children. "Have you forgotten your mother's supposed to be taking things easy? How can I be expected to keep her quiet when you kids keep turning on one thing after another?"

The bitter injustice of this speech stung Belinda into opening her mouth, but the only sound that emerged was a sudden yelp, for beneath the table Robbie's boot had connected smartly with her shin. By the time her leg had recovered, she had control of her tongue. It was really no use arguing with their father, however just the cause. He always managed to come off best.

As soon as it could be arranged, Mr. Barker drove Mrs. Barker, Belinda, and Fanny to town. Robbie had the day off from school and spent it making more rabbit traps and finding new burrows to put them in. Having exhausted all the holes on their own side of the boundary fence, he was having considerable success in the paddock of a badly infested neighbor. He hoped Jack would not find out, for he would consider it foolish in the extreme to be catching rabbits on someone else's property.

The car returned at dusk, and the family trooped into the house with the usual collection of parcels gathered on a day in town. The kitchen table was piled high with groceries of various kinds not available in Bungaree and other household commodities that Mrs. Barker had snatched the infrequent opportunity to buy. The back veranda was littered with tools, slabs of masonite, coils of fencing wire, and cases of sheep dip, rabbit poison, fly dressing, and anything else that had happened to cross Mr. Barker's mind as a possible requirement within the next twelve months.

It took them some little time to get straight and the table cleared for Mrs. Barker to cook the supper. The information they brought with them was that Belinda had strained her eyes, would have to wear glasses, at least temporarily, and would not be able to do any more "close work" than absolutely necessary.

"You will have to go on with school, of course," said Mrs. Barker disappointingly. "So I'm afraid you'll have to give up your sewing for the present—and not much reading, either."

Belinda was not pleased at the idea of wearing glasses. She was sure they would make her look silly.

Mr. Barker was not pleased either. "Why," he boomed

down the supper table to his wife, "when we are all strain-ing every muscle to have *you* sent away and fixed up, must we be constantly having these infuriating additional ex-penses?"

Mrs. Barker said nothing and was not expected to. It did not occur to her to take offense at being referred to as if she were a broken alarm clock. But Belinda, who found it very hard to overlook even the most minor injustice, said in a high, indignant voice, "Well, I couldn't help it. I don't want to wear the beastly things."

"If you can't help it," replied Mr. Barker witheringly, "I'd like to know who else you think can." And with this telling but only partially accurate remark, he won the day.

In the teeth of the instructions both of her mother and of the oculist, Belinda finished the last nightgown. As that source of income would now come to an end, she wished to wring the last penny out of it before it ceased. She was not entirely displeased with her efforts, although she real-ized it would only be a very small proportion of what was required.

Then Robbie, clear-sighted rather than tactful, upset the apple cart. "You know what?" he said one evening as they were returning from their evening jobs.

"No," said Belinda absently, for she was trying to count the eggs.

"You ought to use that money you got to pay the eye man for your specs."

Belinda halted in mid-stride, her jaw dropping. "That's money for Mum," she said at last.

Robbie shrugged. "If you don't pay it, Dad'll have to," he said with cruel logic.

"Well, let him," said Belinda. "I didn't do all that sewing just to get beastly glasses. I'd sooner throw them away."

"You've still got to pay for them," said Robbie. "At least somebody has, and Dad's trying to save money for Mum's hospital, too."

Belinda stamped her foot, jerking the egg tin. "Well, I'm not," she said loudly. "It's my money and I can do what I like with it."

Robbie moved forward. "Just thought I'd tell you," he said. "Of course, no one can make you spend it."

Although Belinda remained fiercely determined not to spend a penny of her money on her own medical expenses, she could nevertheless see the justice of Robbie's suggestion, and it gave her a frustrated and furious feeling. She became bad tempered, shrill voiced, and hard to live with. She was also in the mood to take desperate measures, and this was the reason she fell such a willing victim to temptation the next time she went into Bungaree.

She had sold the last nightgown after having washed and pressed it, had told the lady in the shop that she would be doing no more sewing for her for the present, and had walked out with yet another satisfying pound note in her hand. She was genuinely sorry that her source of supply had come to an end, but she could not be sorry that her bout of sewing was over. By now she was heartily sick of the sight of babies' nightdresses.

She had a few minutes to spare before her mother would be ready to leave for home, and she strolled into the baker's shop to have a word with Sadie. She did not actually tell herself that she was going to boast to Sadie of the money she had made, but it did strike her that it would be nice if Sadie knew.

Sadie had returned from school and was wrapping loaves of bread in brown paper for the mailman to deliver along his route with the mail. She looked up as Belinda entered and saved her the trouble of an oblique approach to the subject.

"I seen some of the things you been making for the baby shop. Gee, they're good." Belinda glanced modestly at the toes of her town shoes.

"Think so?" she said with some embarrassment.

"I seen her sell one to Mrs. Jones over at the hotel, too," said Sadie. Then she leaned a little over the counter and dropped her voice.

"What she give you for them?"

"A pound," said Belinda, not without pride.

"Gee!" said Sadie again. "You must of made a packet." Belinda nodded smugly.

"What you going to do with it?" Sadie then asked.

There was a pause as Belinda cast about for a suitable yet discreet reply. But Sadie did not wait for an answer.

"Know what I'd do?" she asked. "I'd buy a lottery ticket with it. My mum's auntie made a thousand pounds out of the lottery the other day. She's bought herself a motorcar and a TV set." Belinda slowly raised her eyes until they met Sadie's. She did not speak, but her expression encouraged Sadie to continue.

"You could buy lots of lottery tickets with what you got, too. The more you have, the more chances you got of winning."

Belinda found herself saying, "What do I have to do to get one, Sadie?"

"Half a mo," said Sadie. "I'll ask Mum." She disappeared into the back of the shop, and Belinda waited, breathing rather faster than usual.

When she returned, she held a piece of torn newspaper in her hand. "Here you are," she said. "Mum says just write and send the money with it."

"How do I send the money?" asked Belinda. "It won't all fit in an envelope."

"You don't send the cash in an envelope," said Sadie, looking rather horrified. "You got to take it to the post office and say you want a money order for it. It's a bit of paper you put in with the letter; it's easy."

Belinda thanked Sadie with a rather abstracted air and walked out of the shop stuffing the piece of paper into her purse with the pound note. She was quiet during the drive home, and Mrs. Barker was exceedingly kind to her, thinking she was suffering from a headache.

She had intended to rush to Robbie with the information but by the time it was possible to do so, she had lost the inclination and instead decided on a policy of the utmost secrecy. The more she thought about the lottery ticket, the more convinced she became that if ever she were to make any quantity of money, this was the way to do it. It sounded so easy, and Sadie had made it sound so sure. And if a still, small voice somewhere in her interior tried to make itself heard, she refused to listen and was only sufficiently aware that it spoke to keep her plans to herself.

She filled in the form and awaited her opportunity to take it to the post office at Bungaree. This came a few days before the holidays when Mrs. Barker had to visit the doctor again.

Belinda found the transaction unnerving, as she felt sure

the post office official would ask her how she came to own so many pound notes. But he did not, and she walked out of the post office with the money order in her hand. It seemed a very small piece of paper to represent such a lot of hard work. She folded it with the form, slipped them both in the envelope, licked it down, and drawing a deep breath, dropped it into the mail box. As she heard it slither down, she suddenly felt quite sure that she had made a dreadful mistake and would have reached her hand in and pulled it out if it had been possible. This feeling, fortunately for her peace of mind, did not last long, and now that the bold step had been taken and could not be withdrawn, she decided to tell Robbie.

She told him that night when she got home and had the satisfaction of seeing that for once she had really astonished him.

"Lindy!" he said after a moment's mental digestion. "You never!"

She nodded energetically. "I did so. And Sadie says her mother's auntie won a thousand pounds."

"By jings," said Robbie in a hushed voice. "That'd just about do it, I'd reckon."

"Yes," said Belinda. "And that's what she won with only one ticket. I got lots of tickets."

Visions of unimaginable riches floated before their eyes. They almost forgot, in happy anticipation, what they wanted the money for, but while it lasted, it was a magnificent dream. Then Robbie, never quite as sanguine as Belinda, said, "I s'pose it was all *right*, doing that with your money? Say you didn't win the thousand pounds?"

Belinda considered this for a moment, but it was an unpalatable suggestion, and she tossed her head. "Well, we'd be sure to win *something*," she said with confidence. "With all those tickets."

"Um," said Robbie. "But I wonder should you have waited to ask Edward? We could have sent it O.K. in the holidays."

"Course not," said Belinda scornfully. "Why wait? The sooner I send it, the sooner we get it. And Mum may need it any day."

This argument proved unanswerable, and for the time being they let the subject drop, though Robbie planned to tell Edward as soon as he returned.

8: Lorna's Turn

Before Edward returned, they were given something else to think about. A letter came from Lorna by the next mail containing information that surprised them all.

Mr. Barker unlocked the canvas mail bag and emptied it onto the veranda floor as usual, while everyone stood around watching the fountain of letters, circulars, parcels, and newspapers that poured out, ready to pounce on anything that bore his or her own name. This process always caused Mr. Barker intense annoyance, for he preferred to sort the mail methodically and without interruption. But mail was mail, and he had never succeeded in disciplining his family on this point.

Now Mrs. Barker said, "Ah, a letter from Lorna," and bent and picked it up. She took it to one of the veranda chairs and sat down, losing all further interest in the mail. She tore open the envelope, extracted the letter, and bent her head to read it.

"Oh," she said in a disappointed tone.

"What is it, Ethel?" said Mr. Barker, looking up quickly. "Anything wrong?"

"No, not exactly. At least I suppose it's all right." Mrs. Barker, with a worried frown, looked again at the letter in her hand. "She says she wants to spend the holidays with her friend Penny Andrews, and that will be all right, won't it, because we won't be needing her for shearing or anything like that."

"You mean," said Mr. Barker, pushing the big felt hat off his overheated forehead, "that she doesn't want to come home for the holidays?"

"Yes," said Mrs. Barker unhappily. "That's what she says."

"What nonsense is this?" said Mr. Barker, and his voice was like the preliminary rumblings of an erupting volcano. "Of course she must come home. This is where she belongs. What does she think we are? Hotelkeepers or something? Just because she goes to boarding school, she can't think she can go gallivanting off wherever she likes, just as the fancy takes her." The volcano was now well under way, and Edward's dog Spicer, who had just stepped onto the veranda, dropped his tail and his ears and returned unobtrusively into the shrubbery.

"What do you think, Ethel, eh? We can't allow that, can we?" The truth of the matter was that Mr. Barker was just as disappointed as his wife. Robbie and Belinda stood stock still and listened. If Lorna failed to come home, they felt that their whole money-making scheme might fall to the ground. She and Edward were, after all, the organizers of the undertaking.

Mrs. Barker said, "I don't know that we can prevent her, really."

"Can't we?" said Mr. Barker aggressively. "I'll soon see about that. Who is this Pen—Penny Andrews? What sort of a name is that, anyway? And how do we know what she's like? Have you thought of that? How do we know what her parents are? They might be anything. They might run a night club or—or keep a book. How do we know?" He stopped, for here his invention failed. In his bitterer moments city folk, to Mr. Barker, were divided into two classes only: one that ran night clubs and one that took bets on the races.

But Mrs. Barker shook her head. "I shouldn't think they'd be either of those things. Lorna has mentioned her before, and she sounds quite a nice child. I can always write to her parents, of course." She stopped and scratched her chin with the corner of the envelope. "I'm afraid there's no reason why she shouldn't spend the holidays with a friend if she wants to. We'll have to let her go. It's just that —I was looking forward to having her home."

Mr. Barker continued to rumble in a grieved kind of way for a short time after this, but it was as Mrs. Barker had said: Lorna had a perfect right to spend her holidays with friends if she wanted to, and it would have been unjust to insist that she come home. But they were both disappointed. Mrs. Barker wrote to Lorna by the next mail giving her permission to go and asking what clothes she would be wanting.

She intended, also, to write to Penny's mother, partly to put her own mind at rest and partly to make sure that they

really were prepared to have Lorna. But before she could
do this, to everyone's dismay she became sick again and had
to take to her bed.

The truth was that she had not been feeling well for several days, but knowing that Mr. Barker and Jack were beginning to be seriously worried about the drought and the
fact that a recent effort Jack had made to buy in feed for
the winter had met with no success, she had been reluctant
to add a further worry to their already overburdened
shoulders. She told herself that she would feel well again in
a day or so, as she so often had in the past.

That evening as she got up from the table and prepared
to clear away, she suddenly said, "Oh!" and swayed and
would have fallen if Jack had not jumped up and caught
her. She was put to bed and the doctor called once again.
He told them nothing new but said she would have to make
up her mind to go away very soon, and in the meantime she
must stay in bed for a fortnight. She naturally protested, as
she had protested at having Doctor Roberts brought out so
far a second time, saying that it was extravagant and unnecessary as she knew exactly what he would say. But Jack,
in the cross and even rude tone he often used when he was
more than normally worried, said, "You'll stay in bed,
Mum, like Doctor Roberts said. I'm going to ring up Mrs.
Trevor." And he did so, there and then.

The Trevor family, who lived on a nearby property
called Tickera, consisted of four: Sheila, the eldest, who
was at the university; the twins, George and Clive, who
were about to go to the university; and Barbara, who was
Lorna's age and had only recently begun to find her feet
after a childhood hampered by illness. The Barkers had always admired and liked the Trevors immensely.

Mrs. Trevor came over immediately and announced her intention of staying for the fortnight. Mr. Barker and Jack were privately relieved and grateful, and their minds returned to the problems of the drought. Mrs. Trevor wanted to let Lorna and Edward know that their mother was not well, but Mrs. Barker would not hear of this and forbade any letters to be written at all, in case they should suspect that *she* was not writing because she was unable to do so. This was why the letter to Mrs. Andrews never got written and why Lorna went off, in due course, to her job without any of the family having a notion of what her plans really were.

When the fortnight was up, Mrs. Barker left her bed and Mrs. Trevor went home. It was now obvious that the sooner Mrs. Barker could get away, the better. But she refused to consider this, and her husband and Jack could see no way at the moment to insist. Their eyes were frequently on the sky, their tempers were frayed with worry, and to make a remark to either of them was to invite trouble.

To Belinda and Robbie, who were left very much to themselves, their secret plan had never seemed so necessary and important, and they waited anxiously for Edward's return. As a matter of fact, had they realized it, Edward was waiting no less anxiously and with more reason for the arrival of the holidays.

At length the interminable last week came to an end, and, together with a number of other boys, he was put on the train for the west. Lorna had written to him once more before the end of term, telling him that the arrangements had now been completed for her to go to Penny's sister and instructing him to give her love to every dog, cat, horse, sheep, and cow on the place as well as to her own family.

Edward understood quite well how difficult it was for her to do this, but he envied her, too, for she was going to make some money, and so far he had made nothing and still had no idea how he was to do so in the future. He was ready and eager, however, to hear what success Belinda and Robbie had had, and as soon after his arrival as they could unobtrusively slip away, the three of them made off down the paddock to find a secluded corner, and Spicer bounded in front of them, ecstatic and behaving like a puppy because his master had returned.

The first topic to be discussed was, not unnaturally, Robbie's adventure in the mine shaft. He told Edward only the bare bones of it, for he still did not care to dwell longer than necessary on those few hours. But Edward guessed something of what Robbie had been through.

"No one can say you never tried, anyway," he said consolingly. "It was a good idea, and you never know, you might have found something there. Tough luck, that's what it was."

"I got some rabbit skins, though," said Robbie, glad to change the subject. "Thirty-seven I've got ready to sell, and maybe more in the traps tomorrow."

"Gosh," said Edward. "You never got all those on our place, surely?"

Robbie gave him a swift look, and seeing nothing to alarm him, said, "Not exactly. I been over into Jackson's place. There's plenty there."

"I bet," said Edward. "He's a lazy devil." He paused and then said, "You better not let Jackson or Dad see you, though. They're both liable to cut up rough."

"I know," said Robbie. "I've been careful." He turned to Edward with sudden enthusiasm. "You ought to see my line of skins, Edward. They're beaut."

Edward now turned to Belinda. "What about you? Mum said in her letter you been sewing baby things, and I kind of wondered. I've never seen you too keen on sewing before. Did you sell 'em?"

Belinda had been looking forward to telling Edward about her earnings. She felt sure she had made more than any of them and had not been reluctant to say so. But there would be no hiding the lottery ticket now that she had told Robbie, and quite suddenly she began to feel that perhaps Sadie's advice was not the most sensible she could have chosen. Without turning her head she slid her eyes around to Robbie. If he happened not to be listening, she might get away with a half statement. But he was sitting with his legs clasped in his hands and his chin on his knees, and he was looking straight at her. There was quite a long silence, so long that Edward said, "What's the matter? Something go wrong?"

Belinda gave a nervous little giggle, grew rather pink, and burst into rapid speech. "I been meaning to tell you, Edward, but I didn't have time to write, and then my eyes went funny anyway, so Mum wouldn't let me"—she drew a very necessary breath—"I been making baby clothes for that new shop in Bungaree. Lots I made, and she gave me a pound each for them, so I made quite a bit, and then my eyes went funny like I said, and Mum wouldn't let me do any more, and I didn't know what to do to make any more money and then Sadie told me what to do to make lots more without using my eyes at all and so I—and so—and then I—" Her voice trailed off. She looked at Edward with the eyes of a dog about to be bathed and finished in a very whispery voice, "I bought lottery tickets."

"What?" said Edward, leaning forward. "What did you say you did?"

"I—I said I bought—tickets." Now that she had said it, she was sure it was a dreadful thing to have done. She could not bring herself to say it again.

Robbie cleared his throat. "She bought lottery tickets with it, and I don't know should she of."

"Lottery tickets!" said Edward. "What for?"

"We might—win," said Belinda.

Edward looked at her with raised eyebrows and then drew a deep breath. "Oh well," he said with bracing optimism. "They don't cost that much, so you must have some left."

Belinda clapped her hand over her mouth and looked at him speechlessly.

"She's spent it *all* on lottery tickets," said Robbie. "She's got dozens of them."

"You mean, you haven't any money at all out of all you made?" said Edward, and Belinda knew then that she had been foolish, irresponsible, and altogether untrustworthy.

"But I'll win it," she wailed. "I'm going to win it, and then we'll have plenty. Sadie says her mother's auntie did." Her eyes filled with tears, brimmed over, and little glistening channels made their way down each plump pink cheek.

"Course you won't," said Edward. "You silly kid, how many people do you think buy lottery tickets every day? And how many do you think win? Oh well," he said, climbing to his feet. "It's a pity you did all that sewing for nothing, but we still got Rob's rabbit skins. Mop up, for Pete's sake, and let's go home."

It was a dejected little band that trooped up the hill to the homestead. Only Spicer looked in any way jaunty, with his tail high and his nose to the dust, sniffing along imaginary rabbit tracks. The days were drawing in now, and the evenings had a tang to them, telling of frosts not very far away. But no rain had yet fallen, the ground was still hard and dry, and the brittle remains of the spring's grass was all that now covered the naked earth. The rolling hills were like old heads, with the bald patches showing through. The children understood as well as the grownups that if no rain fell before the winter frosts put an end to growth, the sheep and cattle would have a lean time until the spring. And Edward could remember just such another winter when he was small, when not all of their stock managed to survive to greet the spring. That had been a season when all the available grain had been bought up before Mr. Barker knew that he would need to buy in. The passage of time in the country is inclined to be marked, not by great events, but by the kindness or unkindness of the seasons. So they all knew that every penny might be wanted before the end of the year.

During the last week of the term Lorna had sent her address to Edward with the underlined request that he should write to her. Belinda's activities seemed to him a necessary topic to write about, and he did so as soon as the opportunity offered.

When the letter arrived, Lorna had been with Jill and Peter Stevens for approximately a week, and she fell on it as a drowning man grasps at a lifebelt. Edward's rather heavy, still immature handwriting was the one thing she had seen since she arrived that she felt she could completely understand.

When Lorna had had her interview with Jill during the term, there had been nothing to tell her how very different was the life Jill led from her own. Jill was, and had remained, friendly, understanding, and kind. But as soon as

Lorna reached their apartment, which was the day after school broke up, she was faced with a multitude of difficulties.

To begin with, even Jill's appearance she found awe-inspiring. She wore a pair of black trousers with very long, tight legs, ending in a pair of red and white espadrilles. In contrast to the trousers, which emphasized her rather startling thinness, she wore a red pullover so loose and baggy that Lorna felt sure it must have been a castoff of her husband's. A red silk handkerchief was tied around her dark hair and knotted on top, and as a badge of office totally incongruous with the rest of her appearance, she had wrapped a frilly apron around her middle. Penny, who had brought Lorna straight from the school train, bounced cheerfully into the flat and asked where the babies were.

"On the veranda with my darning basket," said Jill. "And I've been praying that you'd bring Lorna soon because if they rummage in that basket much longer, I'll never be able to do another stitch of darning."

The babies, Lorna found, were James, who was five years old and inclined to be solemn, Sally, who was four and extremely lively, and the baby, who now slept placidly in his basket on a table by the big louvred window. The darning basket had been tipped over, and the mess, with half-unrolled balls of wool, tape, elastic, showers of pins and buttons, was indescribable. Mrs. Barker would not have allowed it for a moment. Lorna, without waiting to be introduced, dived on Sally and untwined a pair of scissors from her fat fingers, for they were being waved in close proximity to her brother's eyes. Then she scooped up the pins, salvaged the needle case, and stepped back, her hands full of lethal implements.

"I'm awfully sorry," she said, suddenly realizing that as
yet she had no authority to be saving unknown children
from sudden death or permanent maiming. "I didn't think.
The scissors were so near his eyes."

Jill regarded her with placid satisfaction. "I can see you
have a way with you," she said. "How very useful you're
going to be!"

From the beginning, so far as the children were concerned, Lorna had no trouble at all. She was used to children, and at four or five they are apt to behave very much
the same whether they live in the city or the country. But
other activities that she habitually performed at home without a second thought here presented the most dreadful
problems. Before she could begin to be useful, she had to
learn how to work all the electrical labor-saving devices
the apartment was so lavishly fitted with. Little by little
she got used to them.

If many of the jobs she was accustomed to doing at home
were done here by mechanical means, there were others
for which science had made no provision and which curiously enough seemed to be quite beyond Jill's scope. Darning was one of these; cleaning silver was another; and cooking simple meals for the children was a third. So Lorna took
to cooking for them and picked up the darning basket or
the silver cloth whenever she had a few minutes to spare.
And in this way she began to create order in the Stevens'
home, where there had never been any order before.

She was sitting with the children on the glassed-in veranda one morning, her head bowed over a patch on James's
trousers, when she heard a sound behind her, and she turned
around to find Jill seated on a corner of the table. She had
her eyes on Lorna, and there was a look in them of a kind

of amiable incredulity. Lorna moved quickly and said, "Oh, can I do anything? Did you want me?"

Jill shook her head. "I just came to see how you and the children were getting on. Tell me, Lorna, do you *never* stop working? Do you do this sort of thing at home?"

Lorna put the trousers down and swung around with her arm over the back of her chair. "Well, I help Mum with the mending," she said in some surprise. "But I do a lot of outside things, too." She drew in her breath quickly, thinking with a sudden surge of regret of the old weatherboard homestead, the rambling garden that always needed attention, and the brown, hay-smelling paddocks in which she spent so many active hours. "There's always work to do on a farm," she ended lamely.

"You must miss it," said Jill, looking at her closely.

"Oh, I don't mind," said Lorna, but she did not realize how much her smile gave her feelings away. "James and Sally are so nice to look after," she added quickly.

"We'll have to get you out more," said Jill. "Taking the kids to the park in the afternoons isn't wildly exciting, is it?"

"I don't need to be excited," said Lorna simply.

Neither of them spoke for a few moments, and then Jill said, "I don't suppose you've been to any places much in town, have you?" Lorna shook her head. "Then you had better start by going to the zoo one afternoon," Jill went on. "Penny can go with you."

The look of horror that came over Lorna's face seemed altogether uncalled for until her next words explained it. "But I can't do that. I'm here to work. Why, you're paying me to!"

The trip to the zoo was not easy to arrange, for Penny was hard to pin down. Lorna had been surprised to find

that in the holidays Penny was a very social young lady indeed and was forever going skating or playing tennis or
going to the movies with her very numerous friends. Eventually, therefore, Lorna suggested that she and the children
could go to the zoo on their own.

"But would you really enjoy going on your own?" asked
Jill. "Do you think you could find your way?"

"Oh, yes," said Lorna, whose bump of locality was quite
as good as Edward's and who had never yet been in doubt
about her way home. "If you just tell me how to go, I'm
sure I can."

So in the end this was what they decided. Lorna had no
doubts at first of her ability to get across the harbor to the
zoo and back, and later, when the day drew nearer and she
began to wonder whether she had perhaps undertaken
something that was going to turn out more difficult than
she expected, she felt that she had committed herself too
far to draw back. Besides, it appeared to her as part of her
new duty to be able to get herself and her charges about
the city. So she said nothing and did her best to smother her
growing apprehension.

Edward's letter, arriving as it did in the middle of all
these adjustments, was a most welcome reminder of the familiar life that she missed so much. She joyfully absorbed
every scrap of news, for no mention was made, of course,
of Mrs. Barker's fortnight in bed, but she paused when she
came to the part about Belinda's lottery tickets. She
frowned, peered more closely at the page, as if a nearer
view might alter the meaning, and then read it a second
time. She was tempted to ask Jill's advice but decided not to
when she saw that it would mean revealing too much of
her private schemes. In the end, after much thought, she
replied to the letter.

9: Trouble and Despair

"There! You see?" said Edward when Lorna's letter arrived. "She thinks you're silly, too."

"Well, I'm not," said Belinda furiously. "You're all horrible. I earned it all by myself, and I suppose I can do what I want to with it, can't I?"

Edward shrugged in an irritating way. "If you like making money just to chuck it away, I suppose you can."

"Oh, you go to pot!" said Belinda and flounced off with an unformulated idea of making Fanny uncomfortable, for her temper at the moment was not at its best. Mrs. Barker, worried and with time to observe more closely than usual, was thinking seriously of giving her a course of vitamin pills, which she had been told were very beneficial.

One of the first visits Edward had made when he arrived

home was to the dog kennels. He found all his dogs well
and active, for Jack had been looking after them. Brigalow
greeted him exuberantly. Edward unhooked the chain from
the kennel and took him a little way off. To be on the safe
side, he tried one or two of the orders before letting him
go. The dog obeyed them immediately. He looked about
for Jack, but there was no sign of him, so hoping he was
not making a dreadful mistake that would take him months
to put right, he let go Brig's collar and took him into the
next paddock, where there were some sheep.

At first, underworked and lacking exercise as he was,
Brig was inclined to rush madly at the sheep, chasing them
rather than working them. But Edward kept speaking to
him quietly and constantly as Jack had told him, and bit
by bit he settled down, went more slowly, and fell into
the habits that he had been taught. Edward was very
pleased. Then, as he was tying him up again, he remembered. Fifty pounds was a terrible lot of money, and he
did not really believe what he had said about the pedigree.
He knew quite well that a man who paid that amount for a
sheep dog paid it for the training and not the breeding. He
had made no money at all yet and so far still had no idea
how he was going to do so. The need for money had never
been more pressing, and he felt that the decision he ought
to make was obvious. Having fed them all, he gave Brig a
quick pat and walked away, his eyes on the ground before
him.

The problem worried him more and more. Even Belinda's lottery tickets began to seem preferable to his total
lack of success, though he was careful not to tell her so.
There was Robbie, with his line of rabbit skins in the woolshed increasing all the time. There was Lorna, giving up her

whole holidays to contribute her share. If it had not been largely his own idea, he would not have felt quite so badly. But he should, he thought, be contributing more than any-one else. Again and again his thoughts returned to Briga-low, and each time they shied away. He *could* not sell his dog.

He even paid a special visit to Bungaree to see his friend Garry, the stationmaster's son.

"How could a fellow make some money, Garry?" he asked after the preliminary courtesies resulting from a pro-longed absence had been disposed of.

"I wish I knowed," said Garry simply. He thought for a few minutes and then said, "You got anything to sell?"

"No," said Edward very quickly and firmly.

"Then you got to *do* something," said Garry.

They were sitting on the top rail of the railway freight yard. The back of the stationmaster's garden was not far away, and this was where Edward had found Garry. On either side of them, the shining twin ribbons of the railway line flowed into the sunny distance until they disappeared in wide, liquid curves around the shoulders of the hills. Be-hind the freight yard lay the main street and the huddled weatherboard houses of Bungaree. Only the bank, the hotel, and the gas station stood out clean, rectangular, and self-conscious to speak up for progress and prosperity. In front of them the countryside stretched away for miles, and both of them could have said without hesitation where one man's boundary stopped and another's began. A strong scent, heady and bucolic, rose from the yards at their feet.

"Had a mob of cattle through?" asked Edward.

"Yes," said Garry. "This morning. Ten trucks, Dad said, and all with their sides flapping together. They come from the north somewhere where the drought's worse than here. A drover picked them up. He's taking them out west. I don't know will he ever get them there."

Edward shook his head thoughtfully. "Must be terrible bad up north," he said, "if it's worse than here. I suppose we're not feeding yet, if it comes to that. But there's mighty little to spare in the paddocks. Jack says we will be soon if he can find some." He stopped and scratched his head. "But it's worse out west, he says. I wonder why they'd be going there?"

"Well, south maybe it was," said Garry. "Would there be feed there?"

"There's often a bit among those hills when there's none anywhere else," said Edward. "Could be, but it's not much of a track for weak cattle, I wouldn't think. Glad I'm not him. Did you see him go, Garry?"

"Only the tail end of his dust," said Garry. "I was running home for me dinner. We had a baked dinner today," he added in explanation.

"Which way?" asked Edward, to whom the fact that one should run home for a baked dinner was so obvious as to need no comment.

Garry jerked his head over his left shoulder. "Down the main street," he said. "I did hear they turned off down Bob's Lane."

"That means they'll be going through Trevors' place," said Edward. "And he is going south, then. The stock route to the south goes through their place. I'll likely see him. I got to go over there in a couple of days to get something for Dad, and it'll take him that long to get there."

"If they get that far," said Garry, slipping off the stock-yard rails. "Tell me if you do."

Edward climbed down, too.

"Come down to the creek?" asked Garry hopefully. "I caught three craybobs in the big hole the other day. We had 'em for tea. They were beaut."

"Can't," said Edward regretfully. "I came in with Dad, and he'll go home without me if I'm not there. He never remembers when he's brought someone in with him. Sure you don't know how I can make some money?"

"What are you so keen to make money for?" asked Garry suspiciously. "Your Dad's got plenty, hasn't he? Look at all the land you got."

"Land's no good if it don't grow anything," said Edward. "Anyway, I want it for something special." His face had the closed look of one who could speak if he would.

It tantalized Garry as it was meant to do. "What?" he said. "Go on."

"Nothing," said Edward.

"Bet I know. Bet your Dad's going broke," said Garry, goaded to the ill-advised remark.

"Well, you're wrong, see," said Edward, his face assuming a more animated expression. He took a step forward, and Garry prudently retreated.

"All right then," said Garry from a safer distance. "Why does Belinda have to make things to sell at the baby shop? Sadie says she's been selling things ever since last holidays." He thought that he might have said too much, for Edward looked very angry, and his shoulders hunched a little. Garry was prepared for flight, but his shoulders dropped again as Edward took a deep breath. "You mind your own business," he said.

Garry began to fish in his trouser pockets. "Here," he said at last, pulling his fist out and offering it to Edward.

"You can have this." He dropped something into Edward's hand and Edward saw that it was a sixpence.

"You don't have to give me this," said Edward, acutely embarrassed. He tried to return it, but Garry backed away. "You keep it," he said. "I don't want it, and I'll get another next week."

"Well, thanks," said Edward, putting it with some reluctance into his pocket. "I'll give it back to you after, then." He started to walk away, then stopped and turned. "And I'll come yabby fishing with you one day when I'm in with Mum. What's best for bait? Meat or worms?"

"Meat," said Garry promptly. "Real smelly."

Edward nodded. "Good-o. I'll bring some." He slipped through the fence and hurried back to the car.

Garry watched him till he was out of sight; then he hopped over his own back fence, ran up the garden, and put his head in at the kitchen door.

"Guess what, Mum?" he shouted. "I just give Edward Barker sixpence 'cause he and his sister's trying to earn money, and he's coming yabby fishing with me one day and his Dad's going broke."

"Well, come and wash your face," said a female voice. "It's nearly time for tea."

The events of the following day, however, put all thoughts of crayfishing, or of the drover and his cattle, out of Edward's head.

As far as the children were concerned, all was peace and customary routine until the midday meal. Robbie went around his traps as usual; Belinda, still disgruntled and restless, remained in the house to perform her domestic duties, which she did in a morose and perfunctory way that did not fail to attract her mother's notice; and Edward went

up to the sheep yards behind the woolshed to help Jack with
some drafting. He remained there all morning, for this was
work he enjoyed, and he could immerse himself happily in
it for any length of time. He had Brigalow with him and,
working under Jack's instructions, was introducing him to
the finer points of yard work. He noticed without thinking
much about it that at some time during the morning—
afterwards he could not even remember when—his father
had backed up the big truck to the woolshed loading ramp
and was rolling wool bales and bundles of sheep skins onto
it from the shed. Presently, he heard the engine start up
and glanced around to see the truck rolling off down the
track toward the town. This was such an ordinary occurrence that he thought no more about it. But later in the
morning he was reminded of it again. He and Jack and Mr.
Barker had gone down to the house for dinner and, having
washed and generally made ready, were waiting about on
the veranda for Mrs. Barker's summons to the dinner table.

"Where's Rob?" said Mr. Barker. "That kid has a genius
for being late for meals."

"He's coming," said Edward, who had at that moment
seen him running down the woolshed steps. Afterwards it
surprised him that he had not suspected trouble then, for
Robbie did not customarily run anywhere after he had done
his morning's tramp of the hills.

They were called in to dinner before Robbie had had
time to reach the house. They were all seated, Fanny had
had her bib tied on, and Mr. Barker was helping himself to
salt when they heard Robbie's footsteps on the wooden
boards of the veranda. They approached quickly, purpose-
fully, and heavily, and, contrary to the family's invariable
custom, did not halt at the hall door, where he would ordi-

narily have turned in to wash his hands. They came steadily on to the dining room, the door was flung open, and Robbie entered. Some unusual element in his entrance made them all turn to look at him. He stood in the doorway glaring at his father. His hair was wild, his face was scarlet, and his teeth were clenched. Edward thought, seeing his hands thrust deep into his trouser pockets, that his fists were clenched, too.

"Where's my skins?" he shouted.

There was a silence. Mr. Barker put down the salt spoon, and his eyebrows rose. A sort of quiver appeared to pass over Robbie, and he stamped his foot.

"I say where's my skins?" he shouted even more loudly. The Persian cat crept behind the curtain on the windowsill, and Edward could feel the companionable warmth of Spicer sitting on his feet.

Mr. Barker moved slightly, and the eyes that he fixed on his youngest son were very blue. "Lower your voice, please," he said quietly.

An even deeper color appeared in Robbie's face. He took a deep breath, and the voice that now emerged was as loud as before, but this time it was slightly hoarse and it trembled. "I won't lower my voice. I want to know where my skins are, and you better tell me." He paused, drew breath, and stamped again. "Come on—tell me."

For a moment nothing happened. Edward held his breath, and he knew he was not the only one. Belinda's mouth had dropped open; Jack had given up all pretense of eating and was watching Robbie with his chin propped on his hand. Mrs. Barker had a firm grip on the arms of her chair. Only Fanny was making steady progress through her dinner. Mr. Barker put his table napkin beside his plate and

got up slowly. He pushed his chair back and took two steps toward Robbie.

"Come here," he said.

Robbie, with a face of fury, seemed only too ready to obey, but Mrs. Barker said quickly, "Bill, wait a minute."

Mr. Barker glanced down the table. "What is it, Ethel?" he asked, and they could tell that he was not pleased.

"I—I would like to know what—has happened to his skins."

Mr. Barker appeared to be debating within himself. His brow creased, his eyebrows sank once more, and the evidence of noble wrath disseminated. They knew that the worst was over, and for Robbie's sake they breathed again.

"Since you are kind enough to ask in a reasonable man-

ner," said Mr. Barker in his very best voice, "I am only too happy to tell you they went into town with the rest of the skins this morning. Had Robbie seen fit to ask me this with courtesy and decorum also, I should have been happy to tell him. As it is"—he suddenly swung around and confronted his son—"you will take your dinner and have it in your bedroom. I will not put up with behavior of this kind." He turned and replaced himself in his chair with dignity.

Robbie now lost his temper completely. He stepped up to the table and, with one swing of his arm, swept his dinner plate and its contents onto the floor. There was a kind of splash and a very conclusive explosion of breaking china.

"I don't want any beastly dinner," announced Robbie. "I want my skins back. I thought they were safe in the woolshed. I didn't reckon on thieves getting at them. You stole 'em and you got to give 'em back or else pay me the money."

This was too much for Mr. Barker. He got up again, took Robbie by the arm with one hand, administered one mighty blow on the seat of his pants with the other, and removed him like a piece of damp washing from the dining room.

There was silence until he returned, silence while he sat down, silence until he picked up his knife and fork. Then, slowly and reluctantly, without noticeable appetite, they began to eat. It was Belinda who, later in the meal, plucked up courage to say, "I think Robbie ought to be paid for his skins."

"Yes," said Mrs. Barker quickly. "And I'm going to give him something. But of course he has behaved very badly."

But Belinda was not looking at her mother. Her head was turned to her father, and she continued to fix him with an accusing look. He took no notice until he had finished his pudding. Then he put his spoon and fork together, put the palms of his hands flat on the table on either side of his plate, and lifted his head.

"Why?" he asked.

"Because he caught them and skinned them and they were his, and he specially got them for—" She clapped her hand over her mouth, and her eyes became very round.

Mr. Barker noticed nothing unusual. "And so do we all from time to time," he said. "But none of the rest of us expect special little perks for doing it. Catching rabbits is a normal part of the station work. You all know that. I was glad he was getting his fun out of something so useful, but if I'd known he expected to be paid for it, I'd pretty soon have told him he was mistaken."

"But couldn't you—just this once?" said Belinda. "He's awfully disappointed."

"No, I can't," said Mr. Barker, and they could see he was getting cross again. "I'm not a rich man, as you all know, and I'm trying very hard to gather everything together that I can so that your mother can feel happy about going off for her operation." Mrs. Barker absentmindedly put a hand to her hair. "She'll never go otherwise. And I mistakenly thought I might get a little assistance from you. But not at all." He began to work to a climax, and Belinda shrank back in her chair, for she was neither as brave nor as angry as Robbie. "All I get from you is worry after worry, expense after expense. First Robbie gets himself stuck in a mine shaft and ends up starting a bushfire; then Belinda's eyes go wrong, and we have to have pairs of glasses; then Lorna, who might conceivably be some help, elects to spend her holidays in somebody's house no doubt better appointed than our own. And now Robbie tries to pull the house around our ears because, in the normal way of business, I send the skins into town." He rose to his feet and moved in affronted majesty to the door. Halfway there he stopped by Belinda's chair and pointed an accusing finger at her. "And you, you have been particularly insufferable lately with your tantrums and your sulks and megrims. Heavens above, isn't it enough that I am weighed down by your mother's illness, by the drought and all these financial worries? Do I have to be afflicted by a turbulent and graceless family also?"

As none of them felt moved to answer, he turned and strode to the door. They thought he was gone, but his sense of the dramatic halted him in the doorway.

"Don't think I'm complaining," he said. "My way is to

be silent. But there are times when the very stones must cry out, and this is one of them." With this cryptic utterance he made his departure, and they heard his steps, firm, purposeful, and elastic, down the length of the veranda.

The cat jumped down from the windowsill and took up a new position on the back of Mrs. Barker's chair, and Edward felt Spicer slide off his foot. Belinda started to sob, and Mrs. Barker sighed and said, "Oh dear."

Jack got up and went over to his mother's chair. "Cheer up, Mum," he said. "You know Dad'll be better now that he's got that off his chest." He turned less kindly to his young sister. "And for goodness' sake you shut up, Lindy. Dad's right about you. You have been cranky lately."

A wail greeted this remark, but Jack had gone, and his footsteps followed his father's up the veranda.

Mrs. Barker pushed her chair back and got up. Absentmindedly she walked around behind Fanny, untied her bib, and lifted her down. Fanny trotted off, having apparently noticed nothing unusual during the course of the meal. When she had left the room, Mrs. Barker turned to her two remaining children. Edward sat quietly, his eyes on his empty plate. Belinda's wails were reduced to intermittent sobs, which she muffled in her handkerchief.

"What is the matter with you all?" said Mrs. Barker. "Dad's quite right, you know. You have all been difficult lately. Even you, Edward. I thought you'd be so happy to be home again, but you haven't seemed very happy to me." Edward made a sudden movement, but he did not speak.

Mrs. Barker went on. "It was certainly bad luck about Robbie's skins, but nothing can justify the way he spoke to Dad. I had no idea that any of you would dream of speaking in that way." She pulled out a chair and sat down, and now that the smile had left her face, they could see that she looked very tired indeed. She leaned across the crumby, uncleared table and looked intently at both drooping figures.

"I wonder if you could have got a germ," she said, faintly hopeful. "Or perhaps it's something in the food. Are you sure you are both feeling quite well?"

They both looked up. "Yes," they said in tragic voices, "we're quite all right." And more than this she could not extract from them.

When she saw that they did not wish to confide, if, indeed, they had anything to confide, she got up and began to clear away. "What about Robbie?" she asked. "I should like to go in to him, but I don't think I should, just yet. Edward, do you think perhaps you could—?"

Edward sprang up at once. "Good-o, Mum," he said and, to his mother's surprise, added, "and you better come, too, Belinda, when you've helped Mum with the dinner things."

Half an hour later the three of them were seated on Robbie's bed, and the bedroom door was shut and locked, for Fanny had recently succeeded in reaching door handles. Robbie, rising from the folds of the eiderdown, looked overheated and somewhat moist and swollen about the eyes. He was calm but exceedingly gloomy. Belinda's appearance was similar, though scarcely calm. Edward was speaking.

"It's no good going on about Dad. He was only doing what he always does, and if you didn't tell him about the skins, you couldn't expect him to know."

"But you said I wasn't to," said Robbie.

"I know," said Edward. "And it's a good thing you

didn't, even if he did fly off the handle. What you should have done was to hide the skins somewhere."

"No good telling me that now," said Robbie bitterly.

"I know. I should've thought of it," said Edward simply. "Do you remember how many there were?"

"There were forty-four up till last week," said Robbie. "I'll have to think, though I can't see what difference it makes now."

"Oh well," said Edward. "You never know, and we can get Jack to get the number off the wool-firm statement, anyway. I wonder—" He dropped his chin on his palm.

"What does it matter?" said Belinda. "They're gone. And so's my money. I wish I'd never got those lottery tickets. I'll never talk to Sadie again." And she showed signs of dissolving once more.

But Edward was looking at Robbie in a brooding way, and Robbie was absorbed in his own particular tragedy. Neither of them noticed her, so she swallowed laboriously and maintained her self-control.

Suddenly she shifted her position violently. "D'you know what I think?" she demanded loudly. "I think the whole idea's silly. I wish we'd never thought of it, and I think we ought to give it up. We've been trying the whole of last term, and just look what's happened. My money's gone, Rob's skins have gone, and Edward hasn't made a penny. Dad's livid, Mum's unhappy and still sick, and silly old Jack's horrible. I'd rather tell Mum and Dad what we've been doing and then let's drop it. So there!" she added as a graceful conclusion.

There was a long silence. Then Robbie said defiantly, "Why not? She's right, isn't she?" As Edward did not answer, he continued, "We'd have been better off, even. Belinda's eyes wouldn't have gone bung, and I wouldn't have gotten stuck in the hole or started the bushfire. I reckon we'd better drop it. I'm sick of it, anyhow."

They were both looking at Edward, and they began to think he would never answer. When at last he did, it was only to say in a voice as dispirited as the others, "I wonder should we? We do seem to've just made things worse, don't we?"

"Oh, let's," said Belinda in a more cheerful voice than she had used for some time. "We can tell Mum we tried, and she'll be just as—well, nearly as pleased as if we'd really got the money. You know she will."

"We'd better," said Robbie. "I've caught all the rabbits there are now, and even if I *live* in Jackson's nearly, I'll never get as many as last time."

The thing seemed to be as good as decided, and a load was slipping from their youthful shoulders when they saw Edward shut his mouth tight. "I forgot," he said. "We can't."

"Why not?" said Robbie. "Who's going to stop us?"

"We forgot Lorna," said Edward. "She's staying away these holidays specially to make some money. You know how she hates being away. It wouldn't be fair."

For a moment there was silence; then Belinda said in a voice that would not have melted butter, "You know, Edward, I think Mum would *rather* know the real reason Lorna's staying away. She hates to think Lorna just didn't want to come home."

"And you wouldn't have to even *think* about whether you ought to sell your sheep dogs," said Robbie. It was a blow that got home, and they saw Edward blink his eyes and look down.

"Oh, please, Edward!" said Belinda, suddenly casting diplomacy to the winds. "We can all be happy and nice again and not have everyone thinking we're criminals or something."

For a minute it seemed as if Edward would agree. Then, as if shaking himself free of something, he slid off the bed and stood up, and the concertina'd legs of his old jeans slid down to their accustomed place, about three inches above the ankle.

"Tell you what," he said, and they knew from experience that he had now decided. "Hang on till the end of the holidays, would you? It'll give me a chance to get some money, and it'll give Lorna a chance to get back. Somehow I don't like the idea of telling Mum when she's not here. You don't have to do any more if you don't want to. Even if it didn't work out too well, you did what you could. But just wait a bit. Will you?"

Robbie said, "Oh jings!" and Belinda made mild grumbling noises, but in the end and not with the best of grace they consented.

10: The Drover

Next day Edward caught his horse, untied Brigalow, and set off for the Trevors' property, Tickera, to collect a book on sheep diseases that Mr. Trevor was lending his father. Once or twice Brigalow cantered hopefully toward a mob of sheep and before starting work on them turned and looked at Edward for instructions; but each time Edward called him back. Once or twice, too, he chased a rabbit that happened to jump up ahead of them; but Edward checked him from this also. He knew that a good sheep dog does not lower himself to chase rabbits. Brigalow would have liked to lower himself, though not as much as he would have liked to work the sheep; but he had learned his lesson of obedience well, and after a little time he attempted no more illicit excursions.

Their way led them through their own paddocks to the front gate on the main road. There were three miles of dirt road to travel before they would be turning off into paddocks again, and Edward settled himself comfortably in the saddle and began to whistle. There was very little traffic, for the towns the road connected were small ones. Once a big American car passed him at speed, and from the wire gauze grasshopper-catcher on the hood and the dust that lay thick all over it, he knew it must be a long-distance traveler. Once a Land-Rover trundled past, and the two dogs inside it made impolite noises at Brigalow. This was a local vehicle driven by a stockman or rabbiter going to do some work in a distant paddock. And once the telephone linesmen in their red truck hurried by, and he knew that someone's telephone was out of order. But this was all the traffic he met in the three miles.

Before long he came to a gate, where he turned in. He crossed two small properties before he came to the Trevors' land, and he had not been on it long before he noticed the tracks and droppings of many cattle. Obviously a mob had recently been that way. He remembered his conversation with Garry, noticed that he was now on the scarcely discernible stock route that led through the Trevors' property, and decided that the mob were, in fact, being taken to the rough country in the south. He wondered if he would catch up with them, for if Garry had told the truth, they would not be making very much pace.

But he had seen no sign of them by the time the Trevors' homestead came into view. It lay, serene and welcoming, on the side of a gentle hill with big, sheltering trees in a semicircle behind it. Placed discreetly out of sight of the house

on a flattish piece of ground behind and a little to one side
lay the usual collection of sheds and outhouses, surrounded
by yards and small paddocks. The biggest buildings were
the woolshed and the machinery shed. These, together
with the shearers' quarters, were all painted white, with
red iron roofs. In the yards big trees grew in strategic posi-
tions. The whole effect was one of efficiency and prosperity. Edward looked at it and sighed. He wished he were
bigger and could help Jack, and he did not think it odd that
he should pick on Jack rather than his father.

As he got nearer, he became aware of unusual activity
about the yards. He could see figures moving, and over
everything hung a pall of dust so thick that he could not
see what was making it. He moved in the saddle, and the
pony broke into a canter. If there was any fun going on
down there, then it seemed a pity to miss it.

Fun, however, was not the word they were using at the
yards when he reached them. To his surprise he saw that
the yards were filled with cattle that could only be the
traveling mob. The Trevors had never owned cattle like
these. They were of indeterminate breed but mostly Here-
fords; they were of indeterminate color but mostly red;
and although there were a few well-conditioned, lively in-
dividuals among them, the majority were thin, tired, dusty,
hungry, and dejected. A couple of the Tickera station
hands were moving them in small mobs out of the yards
and into the small surrounding paddocks; the drover's sulky
was standing under an elm tree nearby, with the drover's
dogs asleep beneath it. The drover himself was talking to
Mr. Trevor in one corner of the yards.

Mr. Trevor looked up and waved as Edward rode past.

"Go along in," he called. "Tell 'em I'll be in myself in a couple of minutes." Then he turned again to the drover, and Edward rode on toward the house.

He tied up the pony, made Brigalow understand that he was to stay with it, and went into the garden. It was, unlike the Barkers', an orderly garden, and there were almost always flowers in it somewhere. But this did not make Edward envious as the outbuildings had done. Their own neglected jungle, with its little winding paths and secret places overgrown with shrubs, was more to his taste.

He found Barbara sitting on the front steps greasing a bridle. Rubbing vigorously, she looked up and smiled a welcome. "Hello, Edward. I've been looking out for you. Come on in and have a wash. It'll be lunchtime in a minute."

It was a very adequate lunch, too, because this happened to be one of the periods when the Trevors had a cook. Only Mr. and Mrs. Trevor, George, and Barbara were present, because Clive and Sheila had gone away to stay with some friends.

Mrs. Trevor asked after his mother, and George asked how long it had taken him to ride over, and then Mr. Trevor said, "It looks as if we're going to be stuck with those traveling cattle for a few days."

"They'd better put them in the reserve, then," said George. "Twenty-four hours is all right, but they'll eat the place out if they're here any longer."

"Poor things," said Mrs. Trevor. "I saw them when I went up to the fowls. They look dreadfully hungry."

"That's why they're here," said Mr. Trevor. Then he turned to George. "I hardly like to, with old Bill in a jam. If it was anyone else, I wouldn't hesitate."

"It is difficult," said George. "But he must see himself he

can't leave them indefinitely, and goodness knows how long it's going to take him to replace his offsider."

Mr. Trevor nodded and then said, "What's worse, being Bill, he'll probably insist on moving them himself, and being Bill again, I'll feel bound to insist that he leave them where they are."

"What's the matter with the offsider?" asked Mrs. Trevor.

"Appendicitis," said Mr. Trevor. "That night before they collected the cattle off the train. Bad luck, eh?"

"Worse for the boy, I should think," said Mrs. Trevor drily.

"Oh, he's all right," said George. "He'll be on his feet again in a week. The trouble is they'll never let him carry on with the droving so soon."

"I should think not!" said Mrs. Trevor, whose humanitarian instincts were more strongly developed than those of her husband and son. Their sympathies invariably went to the animals.

"What's Bill doing about it?" asked George.

"He's been on the telephone all this morning," said Mr. Trevor, "and I've promised to run him into Bungaree this afternoon if it'll help."

"Any luck?" said George.

"Not so far, but he seems to think he'll land someone sooner or later. The trouble is there are boys and boys, and some of them are worse than useless."

Barbara suddenly broke in. "Couldn't we help him, just for some of the way? I'd love to."

Mr. Trevor laughed. "I'll bet you would," he said. "And sleep at night under the sulky like he does. And come home with double pneumonia, too. No fear."

"Of course," said George mischievously, "she could earn the money for the new saddle she wants so badly."

"Well, I wish I could," said Barbara sadly. "It's just the sort of thing I like, and the money would be useful." She sighed but not too heartily, for she had not really expected the idea to be greeted with any enthusiasm. However, after she had eaten another mouthful she turned to her father again. "How much would I get?" she asked curiously.

Mr. Trevor shrugged. "Basic wage, I suppose," he said after a little thought. "It's not much for girls your age."

Barbara smiled, but George, who had been muttering to himself, said, "By my calculations it would work out to about six pounds fifteen a week. That's for a boy of fifteen or sixteen, of course, as a station hand; as a drover he might get anything up to nine pounds."

After that they started talking of other things, but Edward did not listen. Little by little as he ate, he became more and more excited, and the more excited he got, the more quickly he ate. And the Trevors, wondering in polite silence why he was so silent and ate so fast, decided that he must be dreadfully hungry. Mrs. Trevor sympathetically plied him with more and more food and absentmindedly he consumed it like a starving expatriate until at last as the scone basket was pushed toward him for the fourth time, he came to the surface, looked up from his plate, and said in some surprise, "No thank you. I seem to have had plenty."

They laughed then, and Mr. Trevor said as he got up, "In that case I'd better fetch this book for your father. You won't want to be late starting back or we'll have your mother sending out search parties. I know."

"What nonsense," said Mrs. Trevor mildly. "But I dare
say it's a good plan if he doesn't waste time."

They all left the table then, and Edward had no chance
of putting the question that had been growing like a balloon
inside him and now must burst. His chance came as he was
leaving. He had slipped the book into his saddlebag and was
untying the pony when George came past on his way back
to the house.

"Hello," said George. "Off so soon?" He smiled pleasantly but continued on his way. "Nice to have seen you
again, Edward. Sorry I can't stop, but I've just thought of
someone I can ring for Bill." He was about to hurry on,
but Edward stepped quickly into his path and said, "Oh,
George, just a minute."

George stopped, surprised and polite.

"I don't want to stop you," said Edward. "But—but I
had an idea. It might help." He paused, uncertain how to go
on and feeling that George must certainly be angry at the
delay.

But George only said, "Oh, have you? I can do with an
idea just now. What is it?"

Edward took the plunge. "Couldn't I go with the
drover?" he asked.

"You?" said George in surprise. "What for? It's going
to cut right into your holidays if you do."

"I want to," said Edward.

"Well, I don't know," said George, obviously taken
aback. "What about your family? Your mother—?"

Edward had always liked George. Quickly he made up
his mind. Then, rather hurriedly, he said, "It's about Mum.
Lorna and Belinda and Rob and me are trying to make

money so Mum can go to the hospital for an operation like
the doctor said. Don't tell, though, will you?" George
shook his head. "I haven't made any money yet, and if he
can't find anyone else, I thought he might take me on. I'm
only thirteen, so I reckoned I wouldn't cost much and he
might." He tried to find an answer in George's expression
but failed. It was an expression he did not understand.

"I see," said George at last, and he looked Edward up
and down. "You're big for thirteen, aren't you?" he said.

"Pretty tough, too," said Edward helpfully.

"Of course," said George. He thought for a moment
and then said, "You'll have to sleep on the ground—take a
swag. There'll be frost probably. Rain, things like that.
Your meals will consist of tea like treacle and a great deal
of tomato sauce, chutney, and pickles with a little bit of
bread and cold meat underneath to hold it together.
Damper, if Bill makes 'em. Sure you want to?"

"Yes," said Edward.

"Come on then," said George. "We'll go and see Bill."

On the way over to the yards George said, "He's a good
sort, Bill. He's often done droving for us. We've known
him a long time now. You'll have nothing to worry about
with him—except, of course, the things I mentioned to
you."

By the time they reached the yards, the last of the cattle
had been drafted off into paddocks, and they found Bill
sitting under a tree with a billy can of cold tea and a piece
of bread, having his afternoon smoko. He was not young
—that much was obvious—but he had one of those brown
lined, timeless faces that could have been forty or seventy.
It had seen so much of sun, rain, and wind that it had set in
permanently protective folds with lines ready at the eyes,

nostrils, and mouth to use for smiling, swearing, or screwing up against the glare. The eyes were deeply sunk beneath
bone and brow and not a great deal of them was revealed
through the half-closed lids, but their expression was not
one of sleepiness. His hat was just now pushed back for
comfort, and a few wisps of lank black hair emerged above
the temple. He wore the usual near-khaki trousers that all
the station hands wore and a washed-out blue shirt, open
at the neck of necessity, for the neck button had gone. Al-

though at this time of day the sun was warm, he still wore a leather jacket. Its surface had the mellow patina of much wear and would quite obviously retain its owner's shape to the last, whether he wore it or not. He was tall and thin and rather loosely put together, so that it appeared as if his purpose were to serve as a hanger for his clothes rather than the clothes being a covering for him. He did not seem in any way weighed down by his predicament but waved the billy with a welcoming gesture as they approached.

"Come and have a drink o' tea," he said. "I got a pannikin somewhere." And he started to fish about behind him.

But George, squatting down against the tree, said, "No thanks, Bill. You carry on. Edward here and I have a proposition to put up to you."

Bill put down his billy, turned, and gave Edward a long, searching, deliberate look. "You have, eh?" he said when he had satisfied himself. "Carry on, then." He leaned back, stretched out his long, thin legs, appeared to close his eyes, and prepared to listen.

"Edward needs some money," began George, slightly to Edward's embarrassment. He understood afterwards that one did not beat about the bush when talking to Bill. "He wants you to give him a job—just till the cattle are delivered. After that he has to go back to school."

"Oh yes?" said Bill, and when it was obvious that he did not intend to commit himself further, George went on.

"He hasn't had any droving experience, but I can tell you, because he won't, that he's quite a useful lad—accustomed to working about with stock and all that. His father's a neighbor of ours, matter of fact. Name of Barker."

Bill picked a piece of dry phalaris grass and began to

chew it. His eyes, very slightly open, were fixed on the distant horizon. Edward began to breathe rather faster, and he could feel something growing tight in his chest. George had apparently said all that he intended to say, for he made himself more comfortable, leaned his head against the tree, and slid his hat forward over his eyes.

At last Bill said, "When can you start?"

Edward gave a jump, gulped, and said, "Now."

Bill nodded slowly, and although there was no other indication, Edward thought that he was pleased. He threw out the dregs of his tea, so that the tea leaves fell with a plop in the dust and a little cloud rose up around them. Then he got up with something of the action of a slide-rule unfolding and said to George, "This here Ed, he's tough all right. He don't even need no swag."

George laughed. "That's easily fixed. I'll pop over to his place and pick it up and meet you on the road."

"Oh gee, thanks," said Edward, for he had forgotten all about his swag.

As it happened, this was not necessary, for Bill decided that by the time all the cattle were mustered again and ready to start, they would scarcely be off Tickera by dark. Edward was told to go home and return at dawn the following day. As he and George walked away, Bill called after him, "Hey! You never told me what wages you're askin'."

After one wild looked at George, Edward shouted back, "Anything. Whatever you say," and then felt it to be a very feeble reply indeed.

But Bill replied, "Good-o, I'll give you a pound a day— and keep. And I'll see you earn it!"

When they were out of earshot, Edward said to George, "That's a lot of money, isn't it?"

But George only laughed. "Don't you worry," he said. "He'll get all the work he wants out of you."

Edward started to thank George and say good-by when they reached the pony, but George said, "Tell you what. I believe I'll slip over and have a word with your mother and father. Sort of break it gently, shall I? Might make it easier."

"Oh, would you? That'd be great," said Edward, realizing at once what a difference this would make. Then he stopped and caught his lip, and an apprehensive look came into his eye. "You won't say anything about—about our plan?"

"Good heavens, no," said George. "I quite understand that's an absolute secret; but I thought I might just tell them what a reliable cove Bill is and that sort of thing. It's what they're sure to want to know—at least, my mother would."

So when Edward arrived home very shortly after sunset, he found the way had miraculously been made clear for him. His mother was, if not exactly pleased, at least resigned and had already begun collecting blankets and extra warm underclothing. His father, while inclined to be huffy that yet another of their flock should apparently prefer to spend the holidays away from home, could not but agree that it was a praiseworthy plan. And to Edward's extreme surprise, he found Jack positively helpful, already planning to lend his own oilskin raincoat, guaranteed to keep water out of the saddle, and full of useful suggestions and advice.

What he did not know was that George had, partly by mistake, broken faith with him. It had been just at the end when George was leaving. He had disclosed Edward's plan to Mr. and Mrs. Barker in the discreetest manner possible and had managed to persuade them that it was a safe and normal thing for a boy to want to do. Then, as he was about to step into the utility truck, he decided that it would not hurt to make one or two suggestions to Jack. He was not sure whether Jack was in the secret or not. Edward, as far as he could remember, had not mentioned him at all. He took a chance and turned, his hand already on the door handle.

"If you've got an hour or so to spare, Jack, it wouldn't do any harm to take a bit of tucker out to them in the truck in, say, a couple of days' time. I didn't want to say anything to put him off. The kids seem to be making a terrific effort to raise this money. But it's going to be pretty uncomfortable and Bill's cooking isn't too hot."

When Jack said, "What money?" rather quickly, George realized too late that he had made a mistake.

"Oh heavens, didn't you know? Well, look, keep it under your hat, will you? I wasn't supposed to have spoken." And, having gone so far, George told him all he knew.

When he had finished, it was quite a time before Jack spoke. At last he said in a thoughtful voice, "That explains quite a lot. Thanks for telling me."

"And for goodness' sake don't let on you know," said George. "I wouldn't like Edward to think I'd let him down. He's a good kid, that."

Jack shook his head. "I won't," he said. "All the same, I'm glad I know."

After that George left, having told Jack which route Bill and Edward would be taking.

11: Edward on Trial

It was dark when the alarm clock ejected Edward from his bed the next morning and almost cold enough for a frost. He had one moment of reluctance before springing out of the bed's warm and pleasant embrace, but as his brain shook off the last clouds of sleep, the reluctance gave place to a slightly apprehensive excitement. He would have liked to be sure that Bill would not be sorry he had hired him, but the prospect of at least a week's camping with such a hardened camper was a thrilling one. Not many excursions of any kind had ever come the way of the Barker children.

He slipped his clothes on quickly and crept along the polished linoleum of the passage to the kitchen. To his surprise a light was coming out of the kitchen door. He went in and found his mother there in her dressing gown. She already had the big fuel stove alight, and it was exuding smells of toast and frying bacon.

"Mum!" said Edward reproachfully. "I said you wasn't to."

She looked up almost guiltily and smiled. "I didn't seem to be able to rest, thinking you mightn't have a proper breakfast, so I thought it would be sensible if I just got up and got it for you and then went back to bed again. I'll still have several hours' sleep after you've gone." She looked very apologetic, and Edward came up and rubbed the side of his head against her shoulder.

"You're a terrible sort of a mum," he said. "But now you can have a cup of tea and some of my breakfast."

In the end he had an enormous breakfast, and Mrs. Barker sat beside him, her bedroom slippers stuck out to the fire, and had tea and buttered toast. In the still and sleeping house, their little feast had a pleasantly illicit air.

He left her finally on a solemn promise not to wash his dishes or to start "just running over the kitchen floor with the mop so it would be dry before anyone started walking on it," and went out into the night.

From the direction of the yards the pony, Blackie, hearing his approaching footsteps, lifted his voice in welcome. Edward had left him shut up the night before, partly so that he would be at hand when he wanted him and partly so that he could give him a large and unaccustomed feed of chaff, bran, and oats. Edward suspected that he would be on short rations for some time to come. The moon had long since sunk below the horizon, and except for the glitter of stars the night was very black. There was no hint of dawn yet and he was glad, for he had a long way to go before the sun rose. A faint breeze rattled the loose pieces of iron on the roofs of nearby sheds, and a little way off an unlatched door creaked from time to time. The breeze had dispelled the frost, but it added its own nip to the autumn night.

He had left his gear ready and under cover the night before, and he made for it now to get his bridle. Out of the darkness Blackie walked up to him, for the pony was not used to being shut up overnight and had been lonely. He saddled up quickly, not requiring light for a job he was accustomed to do almost entirely by touch, anyway. The swag required a little more adjusting and took rather longer. But Jack had showed him how to roll it and strap it on, and it only had to remain on the saddle until he caught up with the drover's turnout. Before long he was ready, the swag across the pommel, Jack's oilskin folded between his legs, saddlebag with knife, pannikin, spoon, and fork on one side, and Jack's own battered black quart pot in its well-worn leather case on the other. He led Blackie out of the yard, shut the gate, and swung into the saddle.

As he started off down the track, the tramp of Blackie's hooves was borne on the light breeze down the hillside to where his dogs were kenneled. In the quiet of this deadest of all hours of the night they started to bark. Hearing them, the other sheep dogs took up the cry, and farther off still the rabbit pack gave tongue. The milker's calf, rudely awakened from his sleep, added his voice, and from the distant fowl yard came the indignant crowing of Mrs. Barker's two cocks. It was anything but a silent departure. However, it reminded Edward of Brigalow, and he pulled up the pony, holding him still while he considered. Brigalow was a sheep dog and not a cattle dog, and it might spoil his training. On the other hand, Jack had said that wherever you went and whatever you did, you should have your dog with you when it was possible, so that he should learn that his place was with you and your horse and not anywhere else.

Edward touched Blackie with his knee and turned toward the kennels. The barking rose to a frenzy. He quickly unchained his dog, mounted again, and allowed Blackie to break into a canter, for the stars, he thought, were beginning to lose their luster. A shadow rushed past him in the darkness, and Brigalow led the way. For the first time in many weeks he considered his dog with unmixed pleasure. He was on his way to earn money at last, and he had no need to feel guilty any more because he owned a dog that could be sold. He left the old house and its sleeping occupants behind and went briskly away across the paddocks.

To his dismay the first of the light became noticeable while he was still on the high road. Blackie was already hot and blowing, but he did not dare reduce his pace. However, there is a longer period than one imagines between the first light and the rising of the sun, and it was still just below the horizon as he rode over the last ridge and came in view of the Tickera homestead. Even from this distance he could hear the lowing of the cattle, and when he looked carefully, he could see that they were just beginning to string out along the track from the cattle yards. The usual cloud of dust hovered over their movements. Bill had apparently had no qualms that Edward might not turn up, for he must have been on his horse at the first split of daylight to have gotten all his beasts mustered and ready to leave by sunrise. Edward went down toward them quickly, and the disturbed, unhappy sounds of the cattle grew louder as he got nearer. From this moment until many days hence, the sound was never out of his ears. And for the rest of his life he could never listen to a mob of cattle without the same sensations as he felt now of excitement, joy, and apprehension.

The last of the beasts had just left the yards as he reached them. Bill, from the back of his own bony bay horse, gave him a swift, appraising glance, which, Edward knew quite well, took in his clothes, his swag, his horse and dog.

"Had your breakfast?" he said in greeting. When Edward had replied, he said, "You know the road out of here to the stock route?" Edward nodded. "Well, go up to the head o' them cattle and see they keep on it, will you? And be sure you keep the track clear of the Trevors' cattle. We don't want to be taking them off to the tiger country we're aiming for. You can drop your stuff in the sulky when we've got 'em between fences. She's not as big as me usual turn-out, but she's lighter for short jobs, and she'll hold all we need." He cast an indulgent eye at his ramshackle, swaying vehicle.

And this was all the conversation Edward had with Bill for some hours. The sun rose, flooding the hills and valleys with warm, yellow light, and the mists of night receded to the creek beds, clinging with failing strength to the tops of the willows until they were vaporized by the increasing temperature of the day. Magpies, confident and sleek in their tidy black and white, began to be busy everywhere, warbling in the branches and squawking in outraged dignity as they dive-bombed one another. Edward could hear their beaks clapping as they did so and was glad that it was not the nesting season when he, or any other small boy, would have been the target for their painful and alarming attacks. Once as he cantered down toward the creek to head off a

roving beast, a pair of ducks whirred into the air and cir-
cled overhead before making off for less hazardous reaches.
Another time a ground lark shot up under Brig's nose, and
Edward laughed to see him jump back and sneeze in surprise. The basket willows along the creek were round and
bushy, for they had been lopped from time to time in the
past to feed hungry cattle. From the amount of dry feed
the Trevors still had on the ground, it was not likely that
they would be lopping this winter; but Jack had said he
would have to lop theirs before long if something didn't
happen. Edward knew this was a last resort, for once the
cattle were fed by hand, they gave up going to look for
their own food.

He stopped and looked back when he came to a rise and
saw the moving mass of cattle stretching away behind him.
At their tail was Bill, sitting in his sulky with the saddle
horse hooked on beside the sulky horse and his two dogs,
one a cinnamon-colored kelpie and the other a broad-
headed, amber-eyed blue roan cattle dog, cantering backward and forward across the rear of the mob. He did not
think there was going to be a great deal of excitement droving these cattle. Most were too poor to show much spirit,
and they were too used to traveling the road. They already
knew what was expected of them, and generally speaking,
they did it because that was less trouble. It was unlikely the
lively ones would try to break away from the others. In
one way Edward was sorry, for cattle work could be quick
and exciting; in another, he was relieved to think the job
was unlikely to make demands on him that he would be
unable to fulfill. He saw a group of the Trevors' steers
some distance ahead standing by the gate through which
his mob had to pass. He called Brigalow and cantered off

to move them before they caught sight of the new cattle
and decided to become better acquainted.

The day was well advanced by the time they reached
the Tickera boundary, and Edward was pleased that they
had gotten through without having boxed any of the Trevors' cattle. He opened the gate, rode out into the apology
for a road that served as the southern stock route, and
placed Blackie in the middle of the track on the northern
side so that the cattle should turn south. They poured
through the gate in a brown flood, and now that they were
under way, their bellowing was reduced to an undertone
of grumbling. The last to go through was the sulky, and
Edward closed in behind it to shut the gate. To his surprise
Bill stopped.

"Smoko," he explained briefly. "They'll do now for a
while, and it's a long time since breakfast." He hooked up
the reins so that the sulky horse could graze about and then
turned the saddle horse loose. They both moved off to the
grass verge and began to pick at the scanty tufts of dry
grass along the gutter. They were old campaigners, too,
and knew what they were about. Edward was going to do
the same for Blackie, but Bill stopped him.

"Better tie him up," he said. "He's too near home, and he
don't know the tricks yet. First thing we know, he'll clear
out, and we'll have Mum and Dad and all the kids after us
because he's arrived home with an empty saddle."

In a remarkably short time, Bill had a little fire going
and the quarts simmering. He had gotten the water from a
battered old milk can that he produced from under the seat
and now poured a cupful into each quart pot. "Boils
quicker," he explained. They sat down with their backs to
a log, and Bill's two dogs flopped down in the shade of a
tree a little way off. Their tongues hung out of the side of

their mouths, and they panted like a pair of little dynamos. Brigalow edged closer, his eye on the piece of bread and tomato sauce that Bill now handed to Edward.

"Send 'im off," said Bill. "You want to learn 'em not to hang round when there's tucker about."

For a moment Edward was defeated, for Brig knew no word that would tell him to go and sit under a tree. He repressed the impulse to get up and tie him up with his belt; it was too undignified. He decided to take a chance.

"Way back!" he shouted and held out his arm as Jack had taught him. Brigalow sprang up and would have raced to the lead of the cattle in a dutiful attempt to bring them back to Edward, but when he had crossed the road, Edward said, "Steady," in a quiet voice. Had these been sheep, Brigalow would simply have slowed his pace, but he had never worked cattle and he was puzzled. So he stopped and turned two pricked and inquiring ears to Edward.

"Sit," said Edward. He had to say it twice, and then Brigalow slowly lowered his hindquarters, still wearing the same puzzled expression. Twice he raised them again expectantly and twice Edward told him to sit. Finally, he grasped that he was to stay there. Bit by bit he moved his front feet forward until his forequarters rested on the ground. He lowered his head, putting his chin on his paws. But his ears remained cocked, and his eyes remained open and fixed on Edward. Bill said nothing, but now he turned, picked up his pannikin, and took a long pull at the steaming tea. Presently he said, "Ordinarily we don't bother with smoko, but we got a long way to go today 'fore the water where we can stop for dinner."

"Good-o," said Edward, who was beginning to think that he habitually talked too much.

In a surprisingly short pace of time Bill had managed to

dispose of the scalding tea. He got up, tossed the wet tea
leaves on to the fire, which hissed once and slowly died, and
walked over to the sulky. Edward began to scramble up,
too, but Bill said, "Take your time," and he sat down again.

Very shortly, however, he threw out the remains of his
tea, for it was both too hot and too strong for his inexperi-
enced palate, picked up the quart pot, and went over to get
his horse. Brigalow, feeling that this movement released
him, jumped up, and Edward patted him as he passed because he had not shamed him in front of Bill.

When they started off again, Edward's swag was in the
sulky, and Bill's kelpie, Ginger, was tied up underneath it so
that he had to run along between the wheels. The sulky was
old and had obviously seen much service. The seat and the
floor were piled high with blankets, frying pans, grid-
irons, and parcels wrapped in newspaper, which afterwards
proved to contain the rations. A hurricane lamp was slung
to the back, where it swung all day long in the dust. Crosswise beneath the sulky was fixed a kind of hammock of
hessian, which contained, among other things, a butt of
chaff for the horses.

The saddle horse was again tied beside the harness horse.
Bill climbed in, settled himself comfortably, and they started
once more. By now the cattle had strung out some distance
along the road and were feeding as they walked. Edward
started off to hurry the tail along, but Bill stopped him.

"Leave 'em be," he said. "They can get a bellyful as they
go. It won't do 'em no harm, poor devils."

So they moved along at a leisurely pace, and in time the
morning passed. The route they were on was no more than
a dirt track, and very little traffic went by. Whenever a car
did turn up, Bill would send his blue cattle dog, Digger,

along the straggling lines of cattle, moving them over onto the side so that the car had room to pass, and the cattle went quietly enough, for they were well experienced. When they came to a cross road or an opening in the fence, Edward would ride through the cattle to the lead and stand there blocking it until they had passed. And once, because they had not been watching, they picked up a stray cow with her half-grown calf that had climbed through a broken fence onto the road.

"Let's see you cut her out now," said Bill, settling himself back in his seat.

Edward rode up quietly toward the cow, edging her over and slowing her speed so that she started to drop back through the mob. Whenever she began to show signs of excitement or alarm, he pulled away until her eyes stopped rolling and her head dropped again. Eventually she found herself right at the tail and cut off from all but her own baby calf by Edward and his horse. She gave an anxious moo and tried to rejoin the others, but he quickly turned Blackie and blocked her. She turned and crossed the road, but he blocked her again, and eventually, when she happened to swing so that she had her tail to the mob with the calf at her side, he turned on her quickly, pressing her forward, and without giving her a chance to swerve back hunted her well down the road. When he rejoined the sulky, Bill nodded approval but apparently did not think it necessary to speak.

Edward had almost given up hope of stopping for dinner when they started down a long, gentle incline and the cattle began to move more quickly. They passed through a patch of scrub at quite a smart pace, and when they came out on the other side of it, Edward saw the reason for the sudden spurt. A wide, full creek crossed the road at the bottom of the slope, and the foremost cattle were already knee-deep in the water, their lower jaws sunk beneath the surface, drinking thirstily. There was a short pick of green grass on either side of the creek, and the cattle would be unlikely to hurry past it.

Dinner was very similar to smoko, except that out of a sugar bag tied around the neck with string, Bill now produced a cold leg of mutton. Taking the meat in his hand and digging in his pocket with the other, he produced a large pocketknife with which he proceeded to slice off a large piece of meat. Having done so, he passed it to Edward.

"Hack yourself off a chunk," he said hospitably.

Following his example, Edward cut what he required, passing back the meat afterwards to be returned to the sugar bag against flies and dust. Each now took a piece of bread, spread it with either tomato sauce or pickles, and the meal was ready. As there were no plates, they held the meat or bread in one hand and the knife in the other and simply sliced mouthfuls off either as required, conveying them to the mouth with knife and thumb. It was a remarkably simple way of eating, requiring neither plate, fork, nor spoon.

When they had finished, Bill pulled over his jacket, which he had thrown down on the ground beside him, rolled it into a bundle, lay back, and slipped it under his head.

"We'll have a bit of a spell," he announced and promptly closed his eyes. Edward did not feel in the least like sleeping but obediently lay down and closed his eyes likewise. To his surprise it was not very long before he felt his limbs relax, his mind begin to wander, and the beginnings of the drift to sleep. It was, in fact, something like ten hours since he had gotten out of bed.

He did not know how long they had slept, but the shadows were just starting to lengthen when they moved on again. The cattle had been resting, too, and were reluctant to leave the creek. This time Bill was on his saddle horse, and the harness horse was left to pull his sulky as the fancy took him. Digger was now tied underneath, and Ginger ran free.

"No sense letting 'em wear themselves out rushin' about," explained Bill. But seeing the way the tied dog raved and pulled and panted without ceasing beneath the sulky, Edward could not help wondering just how much rest he was getting.

Between them they got the cattle started again, and the slow march south continued. This time, riding alongside Edward, Bill was inclined to be a little more talkative.

"Well, how do you like drovin'?" he asked after he had rolled himself a cigarette.

"It's good," said Edward. "I never thought it would be so easy." He glanced up, saw the creases tighten at the corners of Bill's eyes, and knew that he was smiling.

"It's easy enough," he agreed. "All except sometimes. Just sometimes it can be terrible exciting."

"When?" asked Edward, who found this hard to believe.

"I 'member once," said Bill, gazing out at the road ahead. "We was goin' through a town with some young stuff. Up on the northern rivers it was. You wouldn't know. We'd only got 'em the day before, and they was still kind of lively. We went through this town real careful 'cause we knew they was touchy like. And we was gettin' along real well until we come to the show-ground. No one told us

they was havin' a circus that night, and blow me down if
we didn't run clap into a mob of elephants and an old lion
in 'is cage, roarin' 'is head off. I reckon he musta been terrible hungry. The steers stopped dead like as if they was
froze. Then they put their heads up in the air, curls their
tails over their backs, and beats it back through the town
like every butcher in the state was after them. Well—" He
paused and relit his cigarette. "It took us the rest of the
day collecting that mob together again. We was pickin' 'em
out of the funniest places. One got hisself stuck in a kind
of a horse trough thing they had. Another hid hisself under
a heap of grape vines in the bank manager's garden. And
the bank manager got kind of cranky because he reckoned
the grapes was good eatin' and now they wouldn't be no
more. But I dunno, the steer hadn't done nothin' to the
roots that I could see. Then another got hisself wedged in
somebody's kitchen with his head out of the window. How
'e got there I'll never know. You wouldn't credit what a
mess that kitchen was in by the time we got 'im out. And
another I remember thought he'd take a bit of a short cut
and duck through the bulk store of the town's main shop.
They'd been unloading sugar or something and had the
doors open right through. Something went wrong with his
calculations, and he got hisself caught up in some coils of
wire they had there. He didn't half go to market. He kind
of knitted hisself into the wire afore 'e finished and was sitting in a bed o' flour and sugar and molasses and I don't
know what all like a currant (did I mention they was
Aberdeen Angus steers?) in a great big pudding. All the
men had come out of the shop and was dancin' around
tellin' each other what to do. As soon as we showed up,
they forgot about givin' each other advice and went for
us. Anyone'd think it was all our fault! Well, we got 'im

out in the end, but for quite a while we couldn't do nothin' for laughin'. That town was real glad to see the back of us after." He fell silent, lost in the pleasurable remembrance of things past. But Edward was content. At that moment he would not have been anywhere else in the world.

It was almost dark by the time they came to the traveling stock reserve that Bill had been aiming for. They turned the cattle and horses into it, shut the gate, and began to set up camp.

"No need to feed the horses tonight," said Bill. "They'll get a bit of a pickin' in there, and they won't be so lucky tomorrow night."

Bill glanced at the darkening sky, remarked that it was a bit warm for the time of year, and from the hessian hammock beneath the sulky produced a piece of canvas, which he stretched from the back of the sulky to the top wire of the fence, making a low and not very extensive roof. Under this he threw both the swags.

"That'll keep the water out of the blankets if she rains," he said, looking at it with satisfaction.

Considering there had been no rain for months and the sky was perfectly clear, Edward was inclined to think the precaution unnecessary, but he did not say so.

This time he lit the fire and put the quarts on to boil. He tried to make the fire as economical and effective as Bill's but did not think, as he observed the shooting flames, that he had been very successful. However, when Bill came up, he looked at it, nodded, and settled down beside it with every appearance of satisfaction.

Supper was distinguishable from dinner only by the fact that a tin of melon jam was added to the menu. After Bill had rolled and smoked a cigarette, he climbed to his feet,

yawned, stretched, and announced that he was turning in.
Edward was not sorry to do the same, and before very
long the camp was quiet. The fire died down, the dogs,
after a meal of meat scraps and a handful of dog pellets,
found themselves soft holes in the lee of logs or stumps,
and except for the few animals that still wandered about
in search of whatever grass the last lot of traveling stock
had left, all was still.

In this manner and with little or no variation in the pro-
gram, they continued for three days. When the opportunity arose, Bill replenished the stores, but the country was
becoming rougher and homesteads and townships were not
very frequent, and sometimes the bread was as hard as a bis-
cuit. The weather continued fine, but there was a feeling of
change in the air, and every night Bill performed his
weather-gauging ritual and put up the piece of canvas.
After the first night, when he awoke at intervals to hear
Bill snoring and the night wind hushing the higher
branches of the stringybarks, Edward slept without stir-
ring through the hours of darkness until, when the stars
were paling, he would hear Bill grunt, sigh, and clamber to
his feet. They were always on the road by sunrise and
usually in their blankets not long after night had fallen. It
had not yet been necessary to light the hurricane lamp. Edward hardly felt that he was earning his keep, yet Bill
seemed satisfied and apparently expected no more of him
than he was already doing. So he did not let it worry him
but enjoyed the long, slow days and the changing countryside and after a while began to feel that Bill, the dogs, the
horses, himself, and the moving mass of cattle all belonged
to one familiar, companionable entity.

12: A Whistle in the Dark

During this time things were very quiet at the Barkers'
place. With Lorna and Edward away, when they should
both have been at home, with Robbie and Belinda both re-
lapsed into a kind of gloomy petulance and Jack more
quiet and thoughtful than usual, a lot of the sparkle and vi-
tality had gone from family life. Only Fanny remained
unaffected by the debilitated atmosphere, for she found
her entertainment in mysterious and solitary ways that had
very little to do with her nearest and dearest. She continued to trot about in her faded blue jeans, seldom smiling
but seldom unhappy, regarding the world around her
through wide, solemn, remote eyes that took in a great
deal of unexpected detail and could be relied on to have
seen any article lost or mislaid by somebody else.

Mrs. Barker, if no better than she had been, was at least
no worse since her last relapse and maintained her usual
quiet cheerfulness. Mr. Barker, on the contrary, always
affected violently by the atmosphere of his home, was becoming increasingly irritated. One day he returned home
from Bungaree with the flash point of his wrath very near
at hand. He had taken the big truck in for some mechanical
adjustments that were beyond the scope of Jack and had
had some time to fill in while the garage mechanic attended
to it. During this period he had wandered around the
town, making a few necessary purchases and passing the
time of day with some of his acquaintances. News was ex-
changed and various matters mentioned.

Now he burst in at the garden gate, dropped a bag of
bananas as he tried to shut it, picked them up, marched
down the path, stamped onto the veranda, stepped over
Fanny who was busy with some pebbles, dropping another
parcel as he did so, and erupted into the kitchen. He
dropped the remainder of the parcels among the ingredi-
ents of a cake that Mrs. Barker was about to make, threw
his hat on a chair, and placed his hands on his hips.

"You will be interested to know," he announced in a
tone that told Mrs. Barker at once that even if she were interested, she would certainly not be pleased, "that the
whole of Bungaree is seething with the news that we have
gone broke. More exactly, that *I* have gone broke." He
waited, the wiry strands of his white mustache folded over
his lips, trembling slightly with repressed fury.

Mrs. Barker knew that the crowning insult was the "I"
and that she was expected to say something. This was sure
to be difficult. If she made light of it, he would say she was
siding with the traitors in Bungaree. If she joined him in a

simulated rage, it would only add fuel to his wrath. She put the bowl of butter and sugar she was creaming on the table in front of her and gave him her whole attention. After a moment's thought she said matter-of-factly, "But we're not, are we?"

Mr. Barker drew himself up. He was a tall, broad man, and the result was impressive. "Of course we're not," he said.

"Then it can't matter very much, can it?" asked Mrs. Barker gently. "You've only got to tell them."

"Well, naturally I told them," said Mr. Barker with a touch of impatience. "The point is, how did a vicious rumor of that kind start? Who started it? Somewhere in that miserable little town I've got an enemy who won't hesitate to stick a knife in my back. Just as a matter of interest, I'd like to know who it is." The sarcasm in his tone was devastating.

But Mrs. Barker found it hard to believe that her husband had an enemy anywhere. "Who told you about it?" she asked.

"Who didn't, more like it," said Mr. Barker bitterly. "All very tactfully, of course. Let's see—yes, Constable North was the first, when I went in to get some more traveling stock permits. Then the chap in the post office—what's his name? Mullins. Mullins just about wouldn't hand over a dozen stamps till I showed him the money. Nerve! I told him pretty quick. Then—yes, I had to go up to the freight yard to take delivery of that wire, and the stationmaster started sympathizing with me if you please. I thought Jim Smith would have had more sense. I told him so." For a moment his indignation gave place to a fleeting satisfaction.

"Did you find out where they got the information?" asked Mrs. Barker. "That's what really matters."

"Did I now? Let's see—" Mr. Barker rubbed his cheek pensively. "Yes, I did. At least, I remember asking North. I was so taken aback at Mullins and Jim that I never thought to ask them."

"Well," said Mrs. Barker, "who was it?"

"Oh," he answered, in the throes of unpleasant recollection, "it didn't help. He only got it from Jim Smith."

"In that case," said Mrs. Barker firmly, "I'm going to ring Jim Smith and ask him. There's no point in worrying about a silly thing like this when we can fix it up immediately." She wiped her hands on her apron and went out into the hall. Mr. Barker heard the telephone bell ring and his wife asking for the stationmaster. He went off to wash his hands then and did not return to the kitchen until she had rung off.

"Well?" he exclaimed as she came in. She was walking slowly, and if he had been more observant, he would have noticed that her face bore a strange expression.

"He—he doesn't know for sure," she answered. "He thinks—he thinks it started among the children. But you needn't worry. He'll stop it."

Mr. Barker made an explosive noise. "I should just think he would!" he rapped out.

Mrs. Barker picked up the bowl and began to stir. She had thought it advisable not to tell her husband that the stationmaster's information had been that his own son, Garry, had given him the news and had sworn that it was Edward who had told him. She found it very hard to understand and saw no reason why she should repeat such an unlikely statement. All the same, she made up her mind to have a word with Edward on his own as soon as he returned.

That night a telephone call came through from Sydney. Its only purpose was to give Mrs. Barker information, but the information was such that, for the time being at any rate, it banished the problem of Edward entirely from her mind. A pleasant voice informed her that Lorna was being put on the train for Bungaree the following day. In a guarded fashion it mentioned that Lorna was very keen to get home, that she would be a sad loss, and that she would tell them all the news when she arrived. Mrs. Barker was too delighted to ask any questions.

The day that Lorna was to take James and Sally to the zoo dawned clear and sunny and unusually warm. Lorna's fears, which had been growing to a rather uncomfortable size in the last twenty-four hours, were allayed. Nothing untoward could possibly happen on such a mellow, bright autumn day. It was still quite early when they caught the bus that took them to the ferry that would, in turn, take them to the zoo. Jill had given Lorna enough money for their fares and a little over—just in case. They carried only light jackets. At least, Lorna carried them. Sally and James were unencumbered. Now that she was actually sitting in the bus with her charges on either side of her, she felt important, grown-up, and happy. It was all going to be quite easy. All that they had to do on their return was to catch the ferry, then the bus, and remember to get out at the right stop.

After perhaps twenty minutes the bus deposited them at the quay, and they made for the wharf that had ZOO written on it in big letters. After a few puzzled moments

Lorna discovered where to buy the tickets. Then they
went through the turnstile and found the ferry waiting
for them. They arrived at the other side without mishap
and found the entrance to the zoo almost opposite the
wharf.

For a few hours they wandered, engrossed, past the
cages. They remained for a long time beside the seals and
for an even longer time beside the elephants. An alterca-
tion arose about the lions because Sally was frightened and
preferred the monkeys, and Lorna had to leave James with
his nose pressed against the bars of the larger carnivora
while she escorted Sally to the rather smelly monkey
house. They were all duly horrified at the reptiles, and
Lorna, to whom the only good snake was a dead one, was
privately astonished that anyone would waste time feeding

such a collection of bad-tempered and wicked-tongued serpents.

By this time the excitement was beginning to wear a little thin. They had seen by no means everything, but Lorna found that the enthusiasm of her charges was evaporating quite noticeably. Sally said her legs were tired, and James indicated that he was going to find it difficult to prolong life much longer unless he were immediately fortified with food and drink. She took them, therefore, to the restaurant she had noticed earlier in the afternoon. It was quite a walk as it turned out, and they were all very thankful to sit down when they got there. They had to wait quite a long time before anyone noticed them and came to serve them, but eventually they were fed and tempers and behavior improved in consequence.

However, when they came out again, Lorna was alarmed to find that the daylight was, quite noticeably, beginning to go. Also the wind had risen, and a black bank of clouds was rolling up in the west.

"We must go to the ferry now," she told them, "or we shall be late."

"But we were going to see the seals fed," said James.

"And you said we could see the h-h-hippamouse," said Sally querulously.

"Oh dear," said Lorna. "Did I? Well we'll have to do it on our way then, and hurry."

So they did their last two visits very quickly, almost running from place to place. Fortunately for Lorna's peace of mind, the seals had almost finished being fed; otherwise she could never have dragged the children away. The result was that they arrived at the wharf very tired indeed to find that a ferry had just pulled out, and they had to wait a quarter of an hour for the next one.

Owing to these delays, it was quite dark by the time the ferry deposited them at Circular Quay, and the rush hour traffic was at its height. Also the clouds had come down over the city, and a few drops of rain began to fall. Lorna had made a careful note of the place where the bus had stopped and had observed that there was a stop sign for those going in the other direction on the opposite side of the street. She made for it now, grasping the children firmly by the hand, one on each side, and prepared to cross the quay. It was full of rumbling buses, impatient taxis, and homing cars. The headlights were dazzling and seemed to emphasize the darkness in between. She had not thought there were as many motor vehicles in the world as seemed bent on her destruction now. But she saw that other people were crossing, and all of them appeared to escape with their lives. She saw a large, confident-looking man stepping out just in front of her. She took a deep breath, closed her fingers firmly around each small wrist, and stepped off after him.

It seemed to her nothing but sheer good luck that got them safe to the other side, and she let go a long breath of relief when they reached the sidewalk. There were a great many people about, but she managed to make her way through them to the bus stop. Here she received a setback, for a large proportion of the crowd was also waiting for the bus.

"We'll have a little wait, I'm afraid," she told the children.

"I'm hungry again," was Sally's not very reassuring reply.

"I bet we get on first when it comes, anyway," said James even more alarmingly.

They had been waiting perhaps ten minutes when they felt the crowd stir and move forward. One could sense a tightening of muscles. Lorna looked around quickly and saw a large, lighted bus bearing down on them. It looked far more amiable than those she had encountered while she was crossing the quay. She checked that it bore the right number and moved forward with the rest. The bus pulled up with a screech of brakes, and one or two people got off, shouldering their way through the crowd. As soon as the last heel had left the step, the crowd began to flow on as if the conductor had pulled out a plug. Lorna and the children moved forward with the rest, James dragging in front and trying to butt his way through the smallest of gaps.

"Wait, James," said Lorna sharply. "We'll lose you if I have to let go of your hand."

Reluctantly, he fell back, and a number of single-minded, homeward-bound people slid past them. They could see the line of dark figures moving along past the lighted windows inside the bus, and little by little each window became blocked with people. They were still some way back when the conductor moved across the entrance, holding back the crowd.

"Full up now," he said and tugged at the bell.

The bus moved off with its lucky load of passengers, and Lorna and the children were left with quite a number of others to wait for the next bus.

"I told you," said James with a kind of gloomy fury. "We'll never get on if we don't push a bit."

By the time the next bus arrived, the crowd had increased once more. Again Lorna checked the number, and again they moved forward as the bus stopped. But this bus was already half full, and the waiting crowd, seeing this, displayed even more determination not to be left behind. They were all experts at dealing with this sort of thing, and none of them had children to shepherd on board. Once more Lorna was unlucky, though this time she was left on the front line of the waiting crowd. James groaned aloud, and Sally started to whimper.

"We'll do it next time for sure," said Lorna encouragingly. She, too, had begun to wonder if they would ever get home and realized that they were already late.

The third bus came fairly quickly on the heels of the second. It was quite empty, and Lorna knew that all would be well this time. It pulled up with the entrance immediately in front of them, and no one was waiting to get off. With audible sighs of relief the children stepped on and insisted on being taken upstairs. They clambered up, found seats, and thankfully sat down.

"Now we shan't be long," said Lorna.

When the conductor came, she handed him the same amount of money it had cost them to come. He dropped the money into his bag, gave her the tickets without really noticing her, and quickly moved on to the next person. Lorna sat Sally on her knee and put her arm around James.

The rain had been increasing little by little and now fell steadily, turning all the pavements to black lacquer in which the million lights of the city sparkled and danced. It was pleasant to be in the warm shelter of the bus, and Lorna relaxed contentedly, knowing it would be quite a time before she began to recognize her whereabouts. She planned to ask the conductor in good time if she felt any doubts about the right stopping place. In the meantime, she let her eyes follow the brilliant passing ribbon of shop windows and wondered with only half her mind if they were having rain at home and if it were enough to break the drought. Sally, with her head on Lorna's shoulder, was already asleep, and James was in that halfway world where the eyes become fixed and muscles go pleasantly limp. It was not long before he was asleep as well.

It may have been that Lorna, also, slept for a time. She could never afterwards be quite sure. All she knew was that when next she looked out of the window, the shop windows were gone and there were far fewer people and cars in the streets than when they started off. She had that intangible feeling that time must have passed without having been actually aware of its doing so. She glanced around inside the bus. It was now more than half empty. She knew that it had been fuller than this when they started. The bus must have stopped a number of times, and a great many people must have passed her and gotten off without her noticing. She was assailed by a sudden appallingly guilty feeling. Glancing down, she saw that both children still slept soundly. She looked around for the conductor, but he was nowhere in sight. The few people left upstairs were mostly men. Some she did not like the look of at all, but there was one directly in front of her who was puffing at a pipe and who looked quite old, not very prosperous, and not at all alarming. She leaned forward and tapped him gently on the shoulder. Nothing happened, and she tapped a little harder. In fact, it might almost have been described as a poke, for Lorna did nothing by halves. This time the man took the pipe out of his mouth and swung around in surprise.

"Hello, what's up?" he asked in a pleasant, gurgly kind of voice.

"I wonder if you could tell me if we've passed Mansfield Road yet," said Lorna. "I'm afraid I must have gone to sleep and missed the stop."

The man looked a little puzzled. "I'm afraid I couldn't say," he replied. "I can't say I've ever heard of it. I know we haven't passed the junction, if that's any help to you, because I get off there myself."

As Lorna had never heard of the junction and had no idea where it might be, this did not help her in the least. "Oh," she said politely. "Perhaps it's further on then."

The man nodded. "More'n likely. Tell you what, the conductor'll know. Why don't you ask him?"

Lorna looked doubtfully at her unconscious charges. "I

suppose I'd better," she said. "It seems a pity to wake them, doesn't it?"

"It certainly does," said the man emphatically. "Never wake kids except if you're forced to, that's my motto. I'll go and ask him for you. What did you say the stop was? Mansfield Road?" He got up quickly and moved out into the aisle.

"Oh, thank you," said Lorna gratefully. "Mansfield Road. I am sorry to be such a nuisance."

He made an airy gesture with the pipe and sank, rather slowly and laboriously, down the stairs. After perhaps five minutes Lorna saw the top of his hat rising again in small jerks as he ascended. His face, as it rose to eye level, wore an expression of ponderous dismay. He came and leaned over to her.

"The chap says there's no Mansfield Road on this run. Can you remember the number of your bus?"

"Yes, seventeen," said Lorna quickly.

The man pinched his lips together and nodded lugubriously. "That explains it. You're on the wrong bus. This is a twenty-seven."

Lorna's hand came up to her mouth. Her eyes grew round. "I'd—I'd better get off," she said.

"That's right," said the man more cheerfully, as if this decision had taken a weight off his mind. "All you got to do is get another twenty-seven going the other direction and ask the conductor where you can get off to catch a seventeen."

Lorna shook the children gently until their eyes came reluctantly open. "We're getting off," she said. "Come along." In the aisle she stopped. "Thank you so much for helping me. Goodness knows how far I might have gone if you hadn't."

"That's all right," said the man. "Sorry I can't see you off, but my stop's coming up pretty soon now." He turned and settled himself comfortably in his seat, and the last Lorna saw of him was a cloud of smoke wreathing itself around the brim of his hat.

She and the half-awake children moved cautiously down the jerking, bounding bus and managed to clamber down the stairs without mishap.

"I should have got on a seventeen," she told the conductor. "Can you tell me where I can get one?"

"Seventeen?" said the conductor, as if he found the thought quite insupportable. "But this is a twenty-seven."

"I know," said Lorna. "That's why we're getting off. Now I shall have to catch the seventeen."

"Well, you won't catch it here," said the conductor with every appearance of satisfaction. "This is the twenty-seven route."

"Yes," said Lorna, who had had some experience with this kind of conversation at home. "I'm afraid I shall have to go back to the seventeen route. Can you tell me where I'll pick it up?"

"The route, you mean, or a bus?"

"Well, I mean a seventeen bus," said Lorna patiently.

The conductor leaned back against the nickel bar and crossed one blue ankle over the other. "Depends which way it's going," he explained. "To or from."

"From, please," said Lorna. "From the quay, I mean," she added quickly as she saw the conductor was about to pounce happily on this little opening for confusion that he had left himself.

"Well now," said the conductor and scratched his cheek with the ticket punch. "Let's see. You might get one the bottom of Wilbeforce Street, only twenty-seven don't go along Wilbeforce Street now that we've got this new schedule. Then again there's the hospital corner. Does she run that way now, I wonder?" He shook his head sadly. "I very much doubt it. I doubt it very much. Tell you what." He turned to her, and she could see that he had found an answer that satisfied him. "What you better do," he said, emphasizing his words by pointing the ticket punch at her fourth rib. "What you better do is get off this bus and get a twenty-seven going the other way and go back to where you started. You'll pick up a seventeen at the quay easy enough."

"Yes," said Lorna faintly. "Thank you."

At the next stop he helped them off and pointed to the stop on the other side of the road. "There you are," he said triumphantly. "Now you'll be right. But you'll never get a seventeen on this route," he added in a sad and disillusioned manner. He pulled the cord, and the bus moved off, leaving Lorna and James and Sally standing in the dark on a strange road in totally unfamiliar surroundings and in what now turned out to be drizzling rain and a small but chilly wind. As far as Lorna could see, the street was lined with narrow semidetached houses, each with a few feet of garden between it and the road. The street lighting was blue and not very good and turned the faces of the three of them to an appearance of ghostly ill-health. The roar of city traffic came from farther off, but here there was nothing moving of any kind. Only the bus they had just left grew smaller in the distance, its red taillight growing dimmer as it receded. Their one link with familiar things went away and left them alone. Lorna took each child by the hand, and they crossed the road. They took up their position by the bus stop. There was no shelter and no seat. After the warmth of the bus and the relaxation of sleep the children shivered.

"I'm cold," said James.

"I want to go home," said Sally.

"We've just got to get another bus," said Lorna with spurious optimism, "and then we'll be on our way home. You'll see, it won't be long." But now her square, positive little jaw was set, and even the unearthly blue light could not disguise the determined look in her eyes.

It seemed to Lorna that they waited a very long time, but no bus came. Once or twice a car went past, and this raised their hopes, only to dash them again as it came closer. Once a taxi went past, and James said querulously, "Why can't we get a taxi?"

This had not occurred to Lorna, but she was fast coming to the conclusion that some action would have to be taken. She had already put her own jacket around Sally's shoulders and now shivered as much as the children, and she knew that if they were feeling as tired and hungry as she was, which was more than likely, it was time to move. The dismal street began to look as if it had never seen a bus in its life. Lorna wondered if she should knock at the door of one of the houses and ask to use the telephone. But they all looked dark and forbidding, and she thought it possible that they did not have telephones anyway. James's idea now seemed by far the best. But that taxi was the only one they had seen, and it was gone now.

"We will get a taxi," she said. "You tell me when we see one." This consoled them for a little, and their spirits rose a shade. The fact that she had no more money did not worry Lorna. As long as she got the children home, she would willingly go to jail if that was to be her fate.

After another endless period something moved at the far end of the street. They held their breath and watched. The lights came closer, and as it drew near, James shouted, "Taxi!" joyfully. Lorna had no experience in hailing taxis, but she stepped out into the street now with her hand out. The taxi did not stop. It swept past, and she could see in the rear window that it held a passenger. The children burst into tears. She put her arms around them and drew them back to the curb. Sitting down with her feet in the gutter, she put one on each knee and held them tight. Whatever happened, she decided, growing quite angry, she would make sure that Sally and James were all right. She made up her mind to wait another ten minutes and then approach one of the houses. If she had been alone, she would have tried to walk, and even now she began to wonder if it might not be the only way of keeping them warm. But in the dark and during her sleep in the bus she had quite lost her bearings, and she suspected that it might be very much too far, anyway.

Two more cars came past, and she half rose, but she saw they were not taxis and sat down again. The children had apparently given themselves up to quiet misery and lost interest in passing vehicles. Then, almost at the end of the ten minutes she had allowed herself, she saw another vehicle approaching in the distance. She kept her eyes fixed on it, and as it drew nearer, she saw the taxi sign on top of the hood. The fact that it was not alight did not register and, if it had, would have been of no consequence. She put the children gently on the curb and got up. She knew that somehow or other she would stop the taxi. It came closer, going fairly fast. She stepped out into the street and, without really thinking what she was doing, put two fingers in her mouth and took a breath.

Immediately the silence was shattered by a loud, shrill, earsplitting, glass-cracking sound that, somewhere in the distance, started a dog barking. The taxi reduced speed at once and stopped two inches from where she was standing with a squeal of brakes. The front door of one of the nearer houses opened, sending a stream of yellow light into the road. A little farther off a window was thrown up. But Lorna did not notice. She turned quickly when she saw the taxi was stopping, pulled the children to their feet and into the street.

"What's the matter?" said the taxi man, and his voice was a little hoarse.

"You must take us home," said Lorna calmly, and she opened the front door of the taxi.

"I can't," said the taxi man, the hoarseness changing to irritation. "I've got a fare."

"We'll come with you while you take the fare, and then you can take us home," said Lorna, and she lifted Sally onto the seat.

"Here, come off it," said the taxi man. "You can't do that. I've got a passenger in the back, I tell you, and I'm not allowed to take multiple fares." He leaned over, though it is doubtful if he knew what he intended to do, for at that moment James landed on the seat beside Sally.

"I don't care if you have the Queen of England in the back," said Lorna. "You can take us, too. We'll just sit here. We won't disturb him." She slid in beside James and banged the door. "Go on," she said. "Don't be silly."

The taxi man appeared to be unable, for the moment, to find words, but a voice came from the back seat. "Go on, driver. We can't throw children out into the street, you know." And there was a note of amusement in the voice.

Lorna said nothing, the taxi man let in the clutch with great reluctance, and the taxi moved forward. Presently the voice continued, "I wonder if you would mind telling me what sort of noise that was that you made? It was truly startling."

Lorna now turned her head and peered into the darkness at the back. "I only whistled," she said.

"Some whistle," said the voice. "How did you do it? Not in the ordinary way surely?"

"Well, just with two fingers," said Lorna. "My brother taught me ages ago. It's quite easy. We do it so the dogs can hear."

"I am sure they do," said the voice. "I should like to ask you to repeat it, but I'm afraid it might unnerve our driver."

"Well, I'm sorry if I frightened him," said Lorna apologetically. "I didn't really think. I just wanted to be sure of stopping the taxi. We got the wrong bus, you see, and the children are very cold and tired, and I had to get them home."

A kind of snort came from the taxi man, but the voice asked, "Where is home, by the way?"

Lorna started to say Bungaree but stopped herself and gave him Jill's address.

"In that case," said the voice, "we can drop you on the way. We're going past there."

The rest of the drive passed in silence. Now that she had time to think, Lorna realized that she had behaved in a very

unladylike way. She could not think what had made
her speak so rudely to the taxi man and would have liked
to apologize, but there was a kind of frigid silence surrounding him that she felt it would be unwise to penetrate.

The journey was longer than she had expected, and she
was, at any rate, thankful she was not still trying to take
the children home by bus. When, finally, the taxi man drew
up at the entrance to their block of flats, she opened the
door quickly and was about to ask him to wait while she
got him some money, but it was unnecessary. She did not
know that there had been a head looking out of one of the
windows of the Stevens' apartment for the last three quarters of an hour, and now, as soon as it had seen the taxi
stop, it had been withdrawn. Before she could speak, the
front door of the house was flung open, and Jill came hurrying out.

"Oh, Jill," said Lorna thankfully. "I'm so sorry we're
late. Can you please pay the taxi man?"

"The children?" said Jill.

"They're all right, but I'm afraid they're awfully cold
and tired," said Lorna.

Jill heaved a sigh of relief. "Take them up quickly, then.
I'll fix this up and follow you."

Lorna lifted out both half-asleep children, thanked the
invisible voice in the back and the taxi man, hoping he
didn't think too badly of her, and hurried inside.

For the next half hour all efforts were concentrated on
getting James and Sally warmed, fed, and into bed. Nothing much was said until the last blanket was tucked in and
the bedroom light put out. Then Lorna prepared herself
for a bad few minutes. She, too, was cold, wet, tired, and
hungry, and she did not have many reserves left. But Jill,

even now, was not disposed to talk. Lorna was ordered to have a hot bath and get into her pajamas; and with a cold and hollow feeling in her interior, which might have been hunger but which was probably foreboding, she obeyed. Peter she had not seen at all, though she thought she had heard him talking on the telephone as she and the children came in. She decided he was probably too angry with her to bear even to look at her. As she emerged from the bathroom, Jill's voice from the kitchen told her briefly to get into bed. In silence she crept into her room and into bed. She was wondering whether she was expected to put out the light and try to sleep, hungry as she was, when there was a quick step along the hall, an exchange of voices as they passed the living-room door, and then Jill came into the bedroom with a tray in her hands. Appearance can be deceptive, but there was no doubt at all that she did not look angry.

"Sit up, if you're not too tired," she said quite amiably, "and have your supper. You must be quite as hungry as the children." And she put the tray down on Lorna's knees and sat herself on the end of the bed. Peter came in behind her and joined her on the bed.

"We're dying to hear what you've been up to," said Jill. "But have your soup first while it's hot and then tell us."

"And take it slowly," said Peter. "They say a starving man should never eat fast." And his was not the voice of one who found it offensive to look at her.

So as soon as she was able, and with a great weight lifted from her, Lorna told them everything that had happened. In an agony of honesty she told them that she should have left the zoo earlier and that she had completely forgotten to look at the number of the bus before they got on board.

But Peter said, "You can't be expected to think of every-thing. I told Jill it was a tall order for someone from the country like you to do all this on your own."

"It was my fault for letting you go," said Jill. "But you see I knew the children would be safe with you, and of course they were."

She did not tell Lorna what she had already told Peter, that the invisible voice in the taxi had told her, while she was looking for the change in her purse, what methods Lorna had used to stop the taxi and how determined she had been to get the children to safety, no matter what hap-pened. The voice had ended, thinking Lorna was Jill's daughter, by saying, "She's a great kid." Even the taxi man, slightly mollified by the prompt arrival of his money, had said he'd never heard anything like it, and he hoped he never would again. It had not sounded at all like the quiet and gentle Lorna who had inhabited the apartment for the last few weeks. She did look tired now. The healthy, glowing tan of her cheeks had faded, and her eyes, sunk deeply into their sockets, looked darker and bigger than usual. Her shoulders sagged, and her thick, straightish hair flopped over her forehead. When she had finished the soup, she looked up.

"What is the time?" she asked curiously.

Peter looked at his watch. "Just after eleven," he said.

"Eleven!" Lorna looked incredulous.

Jill nodded. "It's been a dreadfully long time," she said, and there was the suggestion of a quaver in her voice.

Suddenly she gave a little gasp and looked quickly at her husband. "The police! I forgot. We must ring them right away."

Peter put out his hand and for a moment rested it on her shoulder. "Relax," he said. "I've already done that."

Lorna stopped eating. The spoon hovered motionless over the soup plate. "The police—?" she said at last.

"Without wishing to be melodramatic," Peter said, and he sounded quite apologetic, "we thought it advisable to let them know that you were—er—missing. But we waited quite a time before we rang them."

"Oh," said Lorna, and she tried to digest the idea of being searched for by the Sydney police. "How—how would they look for me?"

"Inquiring about, I suppose. Broadcasting—"

"Oh dear," said Jill suddenly. "Supposing Lorna's mother heard the broadcast! How absolutely dreadful for her!"

"She'd have rung up, wouldn't she?" said Peter. "If she heard the message."

"She couldn't," said Lorna in dismay. "She doesn't know where I am."

"But you told me she had agreed to let you come," said Jill. "Surely you gave her our address and telephone number?"

"No," Lorna admitted. "I didn't."

There was a long silence. Peter lit a cigarette and seemed to be absorbed in that. Jill painstakingly broke off a loose thread at the edge of the blanket. Neither of them looked at Lorna.

Then Lorna said, "I didn't want to tell her. It was to be a—a surprise. I don't suppose it matters now." And then, because she felt they had a right to know and because she knew they were sympathetic listeners, she told them all about her mother's illness and their plans to make enough money for her to go away. Jill and Peter listened without interruption, and when she had finished, Jill said, "I must ring Mrs. Barker just as soon as Lorna has finished her supper." And then she put her hand on Peter's arm. "Peter—the shack?"

He turned to her and nodded. "Exactly what I was thinking. Just the thing."

"We've got a little place along the coast," Jill now said to Lorna. "It's not very grand, but it's comfortable, and there's a woman who comes and looks after it. If your mother would like to go there for a few weeks—as long as she likes, really—it would be a lovely rest for her and it wouldn't cost anything, and we should be glad to have someone in it. We can't get down very often, and it's empty far too much. I expect, of course, that she'll have to spend a time in some sort of nursing home, but quite likely after that it might come in useful. Would you like to tell her about it?"

In some strange way the tiredness had vanished from Lorna's face. You could not say exactly that she smiled, but she had come to life again. "Yes," she said. "Oh, thank you."

After that they let her sleep, and they knew that she had ceased to worry.

This adventure actually brought Lorna's visit to the Stevens' to an end. Speaking to her on the phone, Jill had realized how much Mrs. Barker was missing her eldest daughter. It took a good deal to convince Lorna that she was not deserting her post by leaving them, once she had made quite sure that it was not because she had gotten lost that they were determined to part with her. In the end she was forced to admit that, although she had come to be fond of them all, home was where she would rather be. There was still a week of the holidays left, and they packed her off on the next available train, making her promise to let them know when her mother would like to use the shack.

As the train slid out of Central Station, she leaned back contentedly, knowing that every click and rattle of the wheels took her nearer home and that in her bag was a check, made out at her request to her mother, for an amount that she secretly thought far more, all things considered, than she had been worth. She did not guess how much they had come to like her nor what a difference her coming had made to the children. She had been touched and surprised to find how sad James and Sally had been to say good-by.

13: Night in the Open

Lorna was so happy to get home that she did not immediately notice the unusual atmosphere of gloom and depression that hung over them all. She was horrified to learn that her mother had spent two weeks in bed and meekly suffered her father's reproof that if she had not chosen to go gallivanting off, she would have been on hand to help; but she was secretly glad she had not had to face the alternative choice. She was more than ever sure that the money she had earned was urgently needed. As Edward was not there, she said nothing, for the moment, of the check in her bag, and if Mrs. Barker wondered what had become of the wages she must now possess, she thought it wiser not to mention it.

Lorna could tell that the drought was still worrying her father and Jack, but there had been a shower a day or so before she arrived, and sufficient clouds were hanging about in that undecided way they do in a droughty period to encourage hope. Things could have been blacker.

The day after she arrived, an event took place of which she knew nothing at the time but which did a great deal to lighten the atmosphere and raise the spirits of at least one member of the family.

The mail had just come in and had been sorted as usual on the veranda floor. Jack had picked up all the business letters and taken them over to the office—a comfortless room that the children were not allowed to enter and seldom wished to. On this occasion, however, Robbie had been sent up by his father with a message for Jack. He went with less than ordinary grace, for Mr. Barker, though quite unaware of it himself, had not yet been re-admitted to Robbie's favor.

Jack was sitting at the untidy desk with papers in front of him and a pencil in his hand. Robbie gave him the message and was about to go when Jack said, "Hey, come here a minute."

Robbie turned and came and stood by his elbow. Jack wrote some figures on a pad, drew a line, appeared to add them up, and then looked around at Robbie.

"The figures have come back from the wool firm," he said casually. "The number of rabbit skins you sent down was forty."

Robbie said nothing, but his brow grew dark and his bottom lip protruded.

"At five bob a skin," continued Jack, "I make that ten pounds." He bent down, pulled out a drawer, and for a moment scuffled in its depths. Then he sat up. "Here you are," he said. "Hop it now, quick."

Robbie took what was offered to him and now looked with open mouth at the two five-pound notes he held in his hand.

"Gee," he said. "Thanks, Jack." Apparently incapable of movement, he continued to stare at the notes.

"No need to thank me," said Jack gruffly. "For goodness' sake put them in your pocket and beat it. You don't have to wave them about for everyone to see, do you? Go on, clear out."

Like a sleepwalker Robbie stepped back to the door and thrust his hand slowly into the depths of his pocket. Once out of the door and down the outside steps, however, the full force of the thing apparently struck him, for Jack heard a sudden earsplitting yell and the sound of swiftly running feet, which disappeared in the direction of the house. He smiled before turning again to his work.

That night the drifting clouds thickened a little and began to look, for the first time in many weeks, as if they might be considering some sort of purpose in life other than a lazy floating in front of every breeze that blew. The air lost its cutting edge and became mild and a little heavy. Hopes and spirits began to rise in the Barker homestead. Only Mrs. Barker seemed unaffected by the change, and this was not because she was unaware of it but because her thoughts kept turning to Edward somewhere out in the scrub with only a raincoat and a ground sheet and two blankets between him and whatever the approaching winter might bring.

Jack had been out in the utility truck two days before with food and had reported all well and in good heart, but he had also said that they were entering fairly rough country, and for some reason Mrs. Barker could never quite explain, this made the threat of bad weather all the worse.

The two drovers, however, were not worrying. Bill was mildly pleased that his prophecies appeared to be coming true, and Edward, except for an ingrained belief that rain, whenever and however it came, was always welcome, gave it no thought at all. Absorbed in his new duties, he had temporarily forgotten how badly the country needed it.

The next day there was a definite feeling of change in the air. The cattle felt it, too, for they were restless and uneasy, and many of them kept up a continuous grumbling as they walked along, occasionally lifting their noses to produce a small treble shriek to vary the monotony. Those in better condition began to put on little spurts of speed, as if they had suddenly become anxious to hurry on but were not quite sure where to. So long as there were no gaps in the fences on either side of the road, this did not matter very much; but it became necessary to watch them more carefully. The dogs were edgy, too, and once or twice Ginger snapped at Brigalow when he accidentally brushed against him.

Several times during the trip Edward had noticed Bill's eyes on Brigalow, and he had wondered whether it was because he considered Brig exceptionally good or exceptionally bad. Brigalow was, of course, unused to cattle and untrained as far as they were concerned. His tendency was to work wide, as most good sheep dogs do, and the quick rush in and nip at the heels that Digger, particularly, excelled at, was something unknown to him. Privately, Edward was pleased that he never attempted it. It might have spoiled him with sheep. But as far as he was able, he was doing his best, and he still promptly obeyed any instruction he understood.

They were traveling in among the hills now. The road was narrow, steep, and winding, and the fences on either side were badly in need of repair. Some stretches of fence were still the post and rail variety of early days. There was very little cleared country, for the steepness of the hillsides made clearing costly and difficult. They would see little open country now until they came down to the river level, by Bill's calculations the following evening. They passed few subdivision fences, for the stock required big areas here to keep alive at all, and the rabbits, having been partly but not entirely exterminated by introduced disease, were breeding up again. There were signs of them about, and also of kangaroo or wallaby. The night before a kangaroo had come silently up to the fire, only to go leaping off in a series of crashes when the dogs began to bark. Edward had just caught a glimpse of its dark, bounding figure vanishing among the trees. Bill assured him that he would see more before they left the hills. Once or twice they saw foxes, with their bottle-brush tails and wide-awake ears. They would not have been frightened of the men, but they ran from the dogs. Occasionally, the tall eucalyptus and wattles opened out in front of them, and they would get glimpses of long blue distances, with the rise and fall of scrub-covered hills stretching to the hori-

zon. Somewhere in the deeper blue folds of the hills the
river ran, but from here it was not yet visible.

There was little for the cattle to eat in this poverty-
stricken sandstone country, and they moved fairly quickly
down the rough road. About halfway through the morning they rounded a corner and ran fair into a large mob of
sheep. They were near an open gate and were being held
by a boy and a dog. They were a thin, wiry, wild-eyed lot
of merino wethers, with less than half a year's wool on
them and very active. Seeing the large herd of cattle unex-
pectedly bearing down on them, the boy and the dog both
flew noisily into action in an attempt to keep the sheep and
cattle apart. But the road was too narrow and the meeting
too unexpected, and all they succeeded in doing was to
alarm the already nervy cattle and start the sheep running
in aimless little darts about the road.

The cattle hesitated, turned, and pushed up against the
fence. If they had been more bunched together, Bill and
Edward would have been nearer at hand and more able
to help. But they were well spread out, and the tail of them
was not yet even around the corner. For a moment the cattle hesitated, and then, encouraged by another volley of
barks from the dog, the two leading steers made a plunge
at the fence. It was in no state to withstand the onslaught
of even a determined rabbit, and in the face of two strong
and edgy beasts it lay down without a protest. A group of
cattle surged through, there was a pause, and then the
sheep, wild and scrub-bred as they were, noticed the way
to freedom was open. A trickle of them, heads down, gal-
loped across the road, leapt into the air as they crossed the
broken fence, and made off for safety and the scrub
whence they had just come. The boy and the dog, concen-

trating on keeping the cattle back, did not notice them in time. The trickle of sheep grew to two, three, four deep, became a flood, and by the time the sulky turned the corner, the greater part of the mob was already fanning out and losing itself down the scrub-covered hillside.

The boy was in a fury of frustration. "Look what yer done!" he screamed. "We been all morning mustering this lot, and now look what yer done!"

The cattle that had gotten through were standing quietly on the other side of the fence, not wanting to leave the others. For the moment they presented no problem. But the sheep, active as goats, timid as wild animals, were bent on putting as much distance between themselves and mankind as possible. Already the first of them were out of sight among the trees.

Without moving from his comfortable position in the sulky, Bill turned to Edward. "Go on," he said. "Let's see what that dog of yours can do. Send 'im after the kid's sheep."

With one look at the fast disappearing sheep, Edward moved his horse forward through the cattle, calling Brigalow as he did so. At the hole in the fence he stopped, made sure his dog was with him, pointed to the sheep, and said quietly, "Brig, fetch 'em back."

After a glance at his master to make sure he really meant it, Brig was off, a black and white streak through the scrub. He bore well over to the right, well outside the most scattered of the still visible sheep, and the last they saw of him was a small, fast-moving dot, appearing and disappearing among the trees. Then he vanished altogether, and the last of the sheep made their way to cover. Bill now turned to the boy.

"Travelin'?" he asked briefly.

The boy shook his head. "I was holdin' this lot on the road while Dad mustered the rest. You can't hold 'em in the paddock. They're too wild, and we got to get 'em out to water."

Bill nodded. "Pretty dry," he commented.

"I'll say," said the boy with feeling. Then he turned and looked, a strange version of Bopeep, in the direction of his vanished flock. "I dunno will 'e get 'em back," he said anxiously. "I'd send me dog but I'm only learnin' 'im, and I don't know would 'e cut a few off."

"Leave 'em be," said Bill comfortably. "I want to see what sort of a job my mate's dog makes of 'em. I don't reckon he'll leave many behind."

Halted by the boy in front and the sulky behind, the cattle stood quietly for the time being. The ones in the paddock picked about at the grass but made no effort to stray far away. Dog and sheep had entirely disappeared, and now that the tramp and stamp of feet had died away the silence of the empty land, with its constant undercurrent of rustling leaves, fell on them. They waited, their eyes on the deserted hillside.

It was perhaps a quarter of an hour later, when Edward was beginning to clench his fists in his trouser pockets, that they saw one, two, and then three sheep walk out of the scrub. A small grunt of satisfaction came from Bill. Two more sheep emerged from a different spot and joined the first three. Then, little by little they all reappeared, panting a little, but not unduly worried.

When a fair-sized mob had gathered and more were still coming, Bill said, "You got a count of this lot?"

"Four hundred and thirty," said the boy promptly.

Bill nodded. "We'll count 'em through the fence after," he said.

Then they saw Brig. He emerged well after the last sheep had come out of the scrub and was trotting quietly up and down behind them, his mouth wide, his tongue lolling, and there was an air of happy, business-like preoccupation about him, as if, at last, he knew what he was meant to be doing and he was doing it with deep satisfaction.

He brought the sheep up to the fence, and Bill climbed down from the sulky. "Let 'em come slowly," he said to Edward, "while I count." He turned to the boy. "You stay here and keep tally."

Quietly the sheep came up to the fence; quietly Edward and Brig forced them on to it until one, feeling too much pressure behind, stepped gingerly across. There was no sign that it remembered having crossed without mishap some twenty minutes earlier. The rest followed him in ones and twos and little bunches, and when the last was through, Bill looked up.

"Four hundred and thirty," he said triumphantly. "That what you make it?"

"That's it," said the boy. "Thanks, mate." He looked curiously at Edward. "You got a good dog there," he said casually.

Edward nodded. It did not seem right for him to speak at that moment.

The boy moved the sheep a little way down the road, and Bill called to Digger, who made short work of retrieving the cattle in the paddock. They had, in any case, decided that their excursion had been a mistake. The feed was no better on that side of the fence than on the road. The problem then arose of how to get the cattle past the mob of sheep without causing more trouble. But this was quickly solved by the arrival of the boy's father with another mob of sheep. The boy's mob was put through the gate to join the new arrivals, and father, son, and several dogs held them on the fence while the cattle went past. He gave the countryman's greeting of a raised couple of fingers to Bill as they went by.

It was while they were stopped for dinner afterwards that Bill said to Edward, "I'd like to buy that dog of yours. You got a price on 'im?"

"No," said Edward reluctantly. "I didn't want to sell him."

Bill nodded and for the present said no more about it, but Edward, with a sinking feeling, knew that this would not be the end. Next time Bill would offer him a sum of money, and he hoped, most earnestly, that it would not be so big that he would be obliged to accept it.

The weather had thickened during the day, and when they started off after dinner, they did so under heavy black clouds and in the teeth of a moaning wind not cold but unsettling. The cattle had given up trying to feed and now moved along bunched together in a manner that made it hard for them to make any pace and harder still for any oncoming traffic to penetrate their closed ranks. Once or twice Bill sent Edward through them to break them up and string them out along the road, but after each attempt by degrees they moved together again.

"It's the weather," said Bill, glancing speculatively at the lowering sky. "They'll be better when it breaks." And Edward noticed that he said "when," not "if."

In this manner most of the afternoon passed. This was to be their last night on the road, for the next homestead they reached was to be their resting place that night and its surrounding paddocks the home of their cattle until the rightful owner was able to feed them once more. Edward looked forward to reaching the day's destination and getting well settled before darkness fell and the rain started. But it was not quite four o'clock when the first light drops began to fall, and because of the clouds the light began to close in earlier than usual. Bill sat in his sulky with Ginger on the floor under his feet, and this time the saddle horse was left to follow on his own because there was little else for him to do and because the only traffic they had so far met that day was the mob of sheep. When the accident happened, it was quite unexpected and they were quite unprepared.

They happened to be going through a particularly thick piece of bush, and the fences were, if possible, a little more broken-down than before. The cattle had crossed a small creek and were making their way up a long, steep hill. The sulky horse was having a drink at the creek, Bill was half asleep, and Edward was sitting crosswise on his horse a little to one side of the mob. They heard the noise simultaneously, and both looked up. A big sheep truck had come out of the bush at the crest of the hill and now bore down on them. It was far too big, one would have said, for the narrow, inadequate road on which it was traveling. Whether the driver was not expecting to find anything on the road and had not seen the cattle, or whether, with the load he appeared to be carrying, his brakes were not strong enough, they were never afterwards sure, but it was not until he was well down the hill and gathering momentum that the truck started to sway as if he were at last applying the brakes, and the horn started to blare madly.

The cattle, still bunched together, stopped, blocking the

road completely. One or two of them mooed uneasily. Bill shouted, Edward straightened himself and dug his heels into his horse, and then at last the cattle moved. They turned and tried to scatter, but it was too late, and the mudguard of the truck caught the first two beasts and hurled them to one side as if they had been sacks of feathers. They made loud, strangled, bugling noises of pain and fear, and this was enough for the rest of the mob. They panicked, bellowing, and the first fifteen or twenty charged over the teetering fence and into the bush. Above the bellowing of the cattle came the shriek and squeal of brakes. Sheep bleated, dogs barked, and dust rose up over the turmoil from the scrambling feet of the cattle. Edward had no time to discover how many of their cattle had been injured or how badly. He only gathered a fleeting impression that the truck had stopped at last when he heard Bill's voice loud and clear over all the other noises.

"Get after them beasts. Don't let 'em get away in the scrub. It's all the fresh ones is gone, an' they won't be stoppin' in a hurry."

Edward wheeled his horse, jumped him over the broken fence, dug in his heels, and made off after the fast disappearing cattle. He did not even know that Digger, also obeying instructions, had raced to the fence after him and now stood, barking and snapping in an effort to hold the breach until Bill should have time to get there.

The escaped cattle were still in sight, but although their crashing progress would be audible for some distance, it would not be long, at the pace they were going, before they were completely lost in the thick undergrowth. Edward's job was to ride around and head them off, slowing them up, calming them down, and by degrees turning them and getting them back to the road. But the ground was rough and full of dead branches, tussocks, yellow anthills, and half-concealed rabbit burrows, and it was all Blackie could do to keep up with them. Farther and farther they crashed into the bush, and the road and all the sounds of the strife and trouble they had left fell farther and farther behind. Edward knew well enough that at that speed one ill-judged step or one concealed hazard could break Blackie's leg and leave him helpless in this tangled wilderness, with probably the cattle gone for good. But he knew it was essential to stay with the cattle, if he could do no more, and so they raced on, twisting, turning, leaping, and dodging as they surmounted obstacle after obstacle.

For the time being he gave up hope of moving around them. He could only hope that Blackie had more wind than the cattle and that, when they had finally exhausted them-

selves, he would still have the energy to round them up and take them back. But they had been badly frightened, and they showed no signs of slowing down. To make matters worse, the day was now definitely fading, the light was already half gone, and the rain was beginning to fall steadily. Edward wondered if, after this headlong flight, they would ever be able to find their way back to the road again. But for the moment all his energies were taken up keeping the cattle in sight and his horse on its feet.

He was following them by sound as much as by sight when he noticed that the ground, which had been falling gently for the last mile and a half, had now begun to rise. It continued to rise steadily and at an increasing angle, and at last it seemed to him that the cattle were beginning to fail. He could feel Blackie's ribs contracting and expanding under him, and he could hear his labored breath, but for all

that, little by little, he drew nearer to the hindmost steers. Their wild gallop had changed to a canter, and this, as the hill grew steeper, to a trot, and when finally he caught them up, their headlong flight was over; they could do no more than walk. But neither could Blackie.

By the time they reached the crest, the cattle had had enough. Apparently, they felt that sufficient distance had been put between them and the terrors of the road. They stopped, heads hanging, sides heaving, strings of saliva swinging from their mouths. Their backs were wet with rain, and in the cooling night air little wisps of steam rose up from them. Edward allowed Blackie a minute or so to regain his breath and then very quietly began to edge him around the flank of the mob. They made no attempt to stampede again. They had quite definitely had enough. But this, though an advantage in one way, became a disadvantage when finally Edward had gotten around to the front of them, for now they refused to move at all, and his efforts to get them started back met with no success. Whether it was the darkness of the night, which now enfolded them, or the discomfort of the rain or the fact that for one day they felt they had traveled far enough or perhaps a mixture of all three, he could not guess. In any event, they were quite obviously there to stay. As if to make this doubly clear, with a sigh and a grunt, two of them sat down; Edward could just make out the dark figures on the ground. He was still wondering what to do when several more lay down, and one by one the others did likewise, until Blackie was the only animal left standing. Edward now became aware that his knees were wet and the water had begun to trickle down the back of his neck. It looked as if it were going to be an exceedingly uncomfortable night.

There now seemed no point in remaining where he was, so he dismounted with the idea of finding a more sheltered place to wait. Now that things had come to a stop, he found that he was stiff and sore and tired and rather cold. Also he was hungry. He was beginning to feel sorry for himself when something colder than his hand and wetter was pushed into it. He bent down and felt, for he could no longer see, and the rough, warm, very much alive hide of Brigalow materialized under his fingers. With his bridle rein still over his elbow, he squatted down, put his arms around the dog, and immediately felt better.

Then he stood up, felt his pony's legs for bumps or cuts or swellings and, finding nothing of consequence, led him over to where he thought he could see a log. It was a tree trunk, with the remains of roots still attached to one end and sticking up into the air. To one of these roots he tied Blackie and was sorry that he did not dare loose his girth or take the bit out of his mouth, for there was no telling when the cattle might decide they had rested enough, and he wanted to be with them when they set off once more. He and Brigalow then sat themselves down on the lee side of the log and got what protection they could from its curving sides. It was scarcely comfortable enough for a night's sleep, but Edward had no intention of sleeping. It was his job to watch the cattle, and this was what he intended to do.

All the same it is a long way through a night, and in spite of the cold and the wet and his determination not to sleep, his head did nod forward more than once and he did sleep for perhaps half an hour or so at a time. But long before dawn his teeth began to chatter and his legs began to get cramp in them. He was wondering miserably whether

he dared get up and move about and risk disturbing the cattle at a time when the utter darkness would make it very
difficult to keep them together, let alone drive them safely
out of the scrub, when they solved the problem for him.
One by one they got to their feet, and he could tell from
the sounds they made that they were poking about looking
for something to eat. Now was the time when they might
scatter past hope of retrieving. With something like relief,
he got up quietly and went over to Blackie. It was better
to move, however aimlessly, than to sit until he was con-
gealed with cold. It was painful to walk, but little by little

it became easier. Blackie welcomed him with a small snuffle, and he rubbed his nose, wishing he had a crust of his dinnertime bread left in his pocket. He mounted, called Brigalow to him, for he did not want the beasts frightened at this stage, and moved Blackie slowly and quietly around the feeding mob. They were difficult to see, and he had to judge mostly by ear. Also, he did not wish to get too close for fear that one or other of them would take fright and, being rested, decide to move on. It was a long, weary, uncertain vigil, and he began to think something must have gone wrong with the sun on this night of all nights. Afterwards, he thought that it was strange he did not think of leaving the cattle and making his own way back. But when someone asked him this later, he merely explained that he couldn't have found his way in the dark, anyhow.

Long after he thought reasonable, there were very faint signs that the celestial organization had not, after all, gone astray, and a pale, watery light began slowly to filter through the trees. The clouds were very low, here and there entangled in the higher treetops, and the rain had changed to a heavy, soaking mist. But hope and courage come with the light, however pale and watery, and Edward turned up his coat collar, pulled his belt one hole tighter, and began to edge the cattle down the hillside.

He had no trouble in recognizing where they had come up, for he now saw that the fall was much steeper on the far side. Mooing in mildly pained surprise, the cattle began to move down the hill. Edward followed them, and as he left the flat ground on the crest, he took one last look around at their night's camping place. Not far from the other side of the log where he had spent the night was a cairn of stones, and he knew that at some time or other someone must have used the hill as a surveyors' post. But trees had grown up now, obscuring the view, and the cairn was falling to pieces. Nevertheless, he noted it as a landmark.

It was not always easy to see which way the cattle had come, and there were times when he had to guide them by guess and by the slight indications Blackie gave of the direction he wanted to go. Even then Edward could not be sure Blackie was not aiming for home as the crow flies. But he trusted largely to his own bump of locality, his powers of observation, and his memory of last night's ride. Every so often he was encouraged by signs of their previous passing. Fortunately, the cattle were hungry now and in no mood to travel fast. He did not expect to come out as quickly as they had come in, but it seemed to him after a time that a great deal of the day was going by. There seemed no alternative to keeping on, and his own hunger and the knowledge that his horse and his dog must be feeling the same kept him moving. By this time he was wet through, and all he could do about it was to try to withdraw from the surface of his cold and uncomfortable body and to live somewhere deep inside himself, ignoring the outside altogether. It was not very satisfactory and needed far greater powers of concentration than he possessed, but it was better than nothing.

They had been traveling for a long, long time, and for hours he had been looking for signs of the road when at last, bursting through a patch of thick scrub, he saw it. Never had he been so glad to see that tumble-down fence and that potholey ribbon of yellow mud as he was now. When they drew near, however, he could see that it was not the place where they had left it, for there was no sign here of the complete break that the cattle had made in the fence. He wondered whether he had gotten his bearings right and whether he should move the cattle up or down the fence, and he hesitated for a few minutes. In the end, he decided to move them southward, hoping to come onto the break and deciding that if, after a mile or so, there was no sign of it, he would make another break and put them through. One hole more or less in that fence seemed of little consequence.

They had not gone very far when the leading beasts started to bellow, and all the cattle began to move more quickly. In a few minutes Edward saw the reason. The break in the fence was only a few hundred yards ahead of them, and two other beasts were standing by the roadside. His own cattle were trotting now. Then they came to the break and went through it in a rush, as if their sole aim for the last twenty-four hours had been to regain the road. There was no sign of Bill or the mob or the truck, and when Edward drew near the steers in the road, he saw that they were limping and guessed that these were the ones that had been hit. He had just made up his mind to continue driving his own mob along the road when he happened to look down and saw that someone had drawn a big and unmistakable arrow across the road. He noticed that it pointed to a boulder. He dismounted, walked over, and rolled it over with his foot. There was a folded piece of paper underneath. He opened it. It said in pencil: "Tried to find you but too dark and mob getting out of hand. I'm taking them on—follow if you find this—coming back with truck to look for you and pick up injured steers. Bill."

He shoved the note in his pocket and rather wearily mounted again. His mob did not want to leave the two sick ones, and he had a little trouble persuading them forward, but eventually with Brigalow's help he got them moving again. He noticed—now that all he had to do was

to keep the cattle moving along the road—that the tops of
the trees and distant stretches of the road had a tendency
to waver and swim in the air, but he still had the power to
keep them stationary if he tried hard. After a time he found
that required altogether too much effort, so he let them
swim and avoided looking at them. Instead he bent his head
and concentrated on the rather worn leather of his pommel and the tangled mass of Blackie's mane.

This was how Bill and the cottage owner found him
when, twenty minutes later, they came along in the truck.
He was swaying in the saddle, so they stopped. Bill got out
and lifted him down.

"Come on, mate," he said. "I'll take over now." And
without wasting more words he took Blackie's reins and
lifted Edward into the front seat of the truck. As an after-
thought he lifted Brigalow in, too, so that he sat, warm and
reassuring, on Edward's feet.

Edward always found it hard afterwards to remember
what happened next. He knew that they must have loaded
the lame beasts on somehow, and he knew that they must
have driven on to the little cottage at the edge of the big
river flat where the other cattle were, leaving Bill to bring
on Edward's mob, but Edward did not really remember
anything else clearly until he woke next morning to find
someone waving a large plate of porridge under his nose.

When it appeared that he had suffered no ill consequences
from his night in the open, he was allowed to get up. He had
known as soon as he opened his eyes that it was raining, for
there was no mistaking that heavy battering on the cor-
rugated iron roof. He thought that they would be starting
straight away for home, but Bill shook his head.

"The creeks are up," he said. "We'll have to wait a couple
of days."

They tried to find out from him what had happened during that night in the open and where he had been. But all he could tell them was that the cattle had kept going until dark and he had somehow managed to stay with them and that in the morning he had been able to bring them back.

"Oh yes," he said at the end. "I remember there was a kind of surveyors' post on the hill where we camped—a pile of stones." The owner of the cottage and Bill looked at one another, and the owner of the cottage whistled.

"That's all o' four miles away from the road," he said in a wondering voice. "I've been lost up that way meself once."

Bill said nothing, but he looked at Edward and scratched the bristles on his chin. "Have any trouble finding the way out?" he asked casually.

"A bit," said Edward. "I wasn't too sure, and I had to guess. We hit the road a mile or so too far down."

Bill nodded. "You didn't do too bad," he said and rolled another cigarette.

For the rest of that day the rain continued to tumble down. No one minded, for it was needed everywhere, and Edward, knowing what it meant to his own family, was very content. He felt languid but none the worse for his adventure. Brig was in fine spirits and was made much of by the cottage owner's wife; and Blackie, who had been very empty indeed when he had arrived, had been shut up in a yard and given as much hard feed as he could eat, for Bill said that too much unaccustomed green grass in that aching void might have disastrous consequences. No further mention had been made of selling Brig, and all, for the moment, seemed well.

It was later in the day that the Land-Rover battled its way into the valley.

14: Grand Finale

The coming of the rain had not reassured Mrs. Barker in
the least. At a time when the rest of the family were exhibit-
ing every kind of joy and high spirits, Mrs. Barker could
only think of Edward and the plight he must be in. They
tried to tell her—at least Jack did—that Bill was an old
campaigner and knew how to look after himself and his
mates, that they must have arrived by now, and that it
wasn't really cold, anyway. But she was not consoled. Although she tried not to spoil their pleasure, her efforts at
good cheer were not very convincing. In the end Jack
drove into Bungaree to find out if there was any news of the
returning drovers. What he heard, from the stationmaster
and his son, Garry, was not what he had hoped to be able
to tell his mother. It appeared that a truck loaded with sheep

had arrived at the railway yard the day before and reported running into the drover's cattle. The last the driver knew before he left them was that the boy the drover had with him had lit out into the scrub on the tail of a panicking mob of cattle. For all he knew, the boy was still in the scrub. He gave them to understand that it was a bad place and easy to get lost in. Garry was popeyed with excitement and importance at being the possessor of such disastrous news. The sheep had been unloaded and had gone off on last night's train. The truck had returned to wherever its home was.

Jack thanked the stationmaster and returned home, deep in thought. As he was about to pass the Trevors' gate, he had an idea and turned in. He ran George to earth mending harness—one of the carefully saved-up wet-weather jobs—and told him. The result of their brief talk was that George sent Jack home to tell his mother that there would be news by the end of the day, and he himself took the Trevors' Land-Rover and went to investigate.

He arrived at the Barkers' place after dark that evening with a very mud-spattered vehicle. They heard his brisk, heavy steps along the veranda and somehow knew that everything was all right. He looked very large and fair and cheerful as he came into the dining room, where they were just finishing supper. He pulled out a chair, accepted a cup of tea, and sat down, spreading his long legs into the only available space left. He looked straight at Mrs. Barker.

"It's all right," he said quickly. "I hope I got the story right; we had to shout across the river. They had a bit of trouble, but they're both at the homestead down there now and Edward looks fine—in the distance, anyway. The rain's holding them up, and it may be a couple of days till they're home."

Then he told them about the accident, how lucky they had been that the cattle got off as lightly as they did, and that, apart from a number who were fairly badly bruised or had cuts and gashes, there were only two that had not been fit to carry on, and even those would probably be all right after a good spell.

"But it seems they've got Edward to thank they're not in a worse mess," said George. And he repeated what Bill had told him of the story: how Edward had tailed the cattle for miles through country that was considered almost impassable, how he had stuck with them all through a cold, wet night, and how he had somehow managed to find his way out with them the next day. He did not mention that Bill had said he was just about at the end of his strength when they found him and would have collapsed if they hadn't met him when they did. But he did end by saying that Bill, that veteran of bushcraft, had said he'd never seen anyone who was Edward's equal for perseverance and sense of direction. "Bill actually said," he finished, " 'That Ed, he's bung full o' guts and you couldn't lose 'im if you tried.' And it took him quite a bit to say it, for he was hoarse as a crow from shouting the whole story to me across the river." He sat back and drank his tea.

Mrs. Barker held her teacup, too, but its contents were gently splashing into her bread-and-butter plate, for her eyes were fixed on George, and she wore a sort of half smile that George found adequate compensation for the long trip he had taken that day.

After thirty-six hours the rain eased off, the creeks went down, and the earth gratefully soaked up its two or three inches. Bill and Edward harnessed up the sulky horse, saddled the other two, collected the dogs, and said good-by to their hosts. In a glistening, trickling, sparkling world they made their way up the long, rough hill to civilization. Sometimes Edward rode, and sometimes he sat in the sulky with Bill, and Blackie followed behind with Bill's saddle horse. Bill was more talkative now and told Edward stories of droving out west and up in the territory that made Edward wish he were a few years older and with his tedious school-time behind him. But there came a time when Bill ran out of stories, and they sat silent while the horses clop-clopped along on the wet gravel and the wheels crackled and splashed behind the sulky horse's bobbing rump. Brigalow was cantering along ahead with Digger, and Edward could see that Bill was watching him. At last he took out the butt of the cigarette he had been smoking and dropped it carefully in a passing puddle.

"If you *was* thinking of selling that dog," he said in a thoughtful kind of way, "I'd give you fifty pound for him."

There was a long, long silence. Bill's eyes slid around quickly to Edward and away again. Edward's face was red, and he seemed to be staring down at his hands.

"O' course," said Bill, when Edward had failed to answer after a considerable time. "I know how it is with a fellow and his dog, and likely you don't want to part with 'im, but from something George Trevor said, I got the idea you was a bit shy of cash, and I thought I'd mention it. He's a good dog, that. I like the cut of him."

Still Edward said nothing, but the small movement of his hands in his lap was almost as if he were wringing them. Then, suddenly, they were still. His head went up, his eyes flew open, and an altogether different expression came over his face. He turned now to Bill.

"I couldn't turn that much money down," he said simply.

"But if—if you weren't fussy exactly which dog you had, Brig's got two brothers and a sister at home, same age. They aren't trained yet, but—but you could have them all for fifty pounds." For all its eagerness there was something desperate in his expression. His fingers now grasped his knees until the knucklebones showed through white. Then, as he continued to stare into Bill's face, he saw the wrinkles around his eyes screw up. The lean mouth twitched, and Edward's fingers slowly relaxed.

"I'd have to look at 'em of course," said Bill.

"Of course," said Edward.

And that was why, when Edward rode home at the end of the following day, Bill and his sulky and his saddle horse and Ginger and Digger came with him. And before he as much as entered the garden gate, he took Bill to the kennels. He got off Blackie and threw the reins over the stock-yard post, and Bill clambered stiffly down from the sulky. Their dogs flopped down where they were, their noses on their paws. For quite a time Bill and Edward squatted, first by one kennel and then by another. One by one Brigalow's brothers and sisters were let off to run around, were patted, handled, rolled over, and every movement, every expression, studied. At last Bill got up.

"I'll take the dog with the white foot," he said.

"But—but what about the others?" asked Edward.

Deep in the lined brown face Bill's eyes twinkled. "I couldn't use no more than one," he said, and as Edward's face began to fall, added, drawling, "but I'll pay yer what I said. I can see he's a good 'un, and if you was to look after the other two careful, I might be able to sell 'em for yer, too. I know one or two who's lookin' out for a dog. That's if you want to, of course."

"Yes," said Edward quickly. "I wouldn't mind doing that."

"On second thoughts," said Bill. "D'yer know, if I was you, I'd keep the bitch. If these ones turn out any good, it might be useful to know there was more like 'em. O.K., mate?"

"O.K.," said Edward.

After that Bill went. First he took the dog, put him in a chaff bag, and laid him gently on the floor of the sulky. Then he laboriously wrote out a check, which he handed to Edward, explaining that it was for the droving as well as for the dog. He wouldn't come up to the house, but before he climbed into the sulky, he put his wiry, knobbled hand on Edward's shoulder and shook it gently.

"You look after yourself now, mate. You've got a little bit to go yet before you're properly growed up, and you don't want to go knocking yourself about." He climbed in, slapped the reins on the horse's rump, and called his dogs. The sulky trundled down the track with Bill's long, thin form swaying and leaning to the bumps, the saddle horse companionably jogging along beside the sulky horse, and the two dogs loping along side by side behind. Edward watched for a few minutes and then glanced down at the check in his hand. He gasped and opened his mouth to call out. But the sulky was now small in the distance, and he knew that Bill would not hear. Thoughtfully, he folded the check, put it in his pocket, and after letting Blackie go, walked slowly up to the house.

Even now, so soon after the rain, there was a different feel about the place. It was too soon for the new shoots to show, and more rain would be needed still; but the drought had broken, the rain had come at last, and under the ground a million, million little seeds were beginning to germinate. Nursery showers, Edward thought. That's all that's needed now.

The family had not heard him come and had not, in fact, expected him until the following day. They were all in, reading the mail and the papers and waiting for their supper to appear.

Edward walked into the kitchen, and as he did so, his mother looked up from the stove. Her face lit up immediately.

"Edward!" she exclaimed. "What a lovely surprise!" she turned and called, "Lorna! Lorna! Lay a place for Edward. He's back." And then they all trooped into the kitchen, Fanny, Belinda, Robbie, Lorna, Jack, and even Mr. Barker, and on all their faces was the same look of delighted surprise that he had seen on his mother's. He found it a trifle overwhelming but deeply satisfying.

Supper was a riotous and cheerful meal. Only Fanny and Mrs. Barker had not quite the same hilarious spirit as the others—Fanny because she was still just Fanny, and Mrs. Barker because, although she had her family gathered around her once more, she was still privately puzzling over various unexplained matters. Mr. Barker might have been puzzled over them, too, but the advent of the rain had altered his outlook completely. Details were now overlooked, small misdemeanors no longer mattered, and they all basked in the rather dazzling sunshine of his approval and general good spirits.

After the supper was cleared away and washed up and before the edict for bed went forth, all the children mysteriously vanished, and a solemn conference took place in the girls' bedroom. Of the four of them, it now appeared that three had been successful, and only Belinda, who threatened to dissolve in a tearful heap, had nothing to show for her three months' effort. Lorna told the others about the offer of the Stevens' cottage, and they all agreed that this was a master stroke. The question now was whether to present Mrs. Barker with the checks and cash and the offer of the cottage and tell her the sad fate of Belinda's earnings, or to wait a few days in the faint hope that Belinda's frail bark might come home.

"When's the lottery drawn?" asked Edward.

They looked blankly at one another. "I never thought to ask," said Belinda.

"She might," said Robbie. "She still just might."

"Oh, wait till I ask Sadie," said Belinda. "Please, please, wait."

So reluctantly, because there were only a few days left, they decided to wait till after the next visit to town. They were dispersing in the furtive manner of conspirators when there came a little rustle from beneath the bed, and to their consternation Fanny crawled forth. There was no expression at all on her face. The four desperate plotters pounced on her, held her firmly, and made her promise under threat of the most dreadful penalties not to tell a Single Soul. When they felt they could do no more, they let her go and watched with serious misgivings as she pattered down the hall. There was no telling with Fanny whether she had understood what they had been saying or not.

Two days later they went into town. They all went but Jack, and the car was very full. In Bungaree they went off on their own separate affairs. Mrs. Barker had to visit the doctor again, and Mr. Barker wished to pay a visit to the bank. Belinda, in charge of Fanny, went off to interview

Sadie, and the other three started on the list of shopping Mrs. Barker had given them.

It was perhaps an hour later when Edward, Lorna, and Robbie again encountered Belinda. Her face was flushed, her eyes were blazing, and she could scarcely articulate. She came running toward them. Her first words were surprising.

"Let's go home," she said. "Oh, let's go home quickly."

Edward looked her over and said, "What's up? Feeling sick?"

Belinda gave him one swift, scornful look and said, "The mail will have come when we get back, and I must see— Sadie says she's *sure* she saw in the paper yesterday one of my numbers has won something. She's been going to get her mum to ring, she says, but there'll be a letter in the mail today if it has. Oh, can't we hurry?" Belinda drew a long and badly needed breath.

Lorna was beginning to look suitably impressed, but Robbie said, "How does she know what your numbers are, anyway?"

"I told her," said Belinda. "When I got them, I gave her the list, 'cause she could tell me if they were lucky."

"Were they?" asked Edward.

"She—she didn't know. But, oh, they must have been. Couldn't we go home now?" She looked around rather wildly, but there was no sign yet of Mr. and Mrs. Barker. They all moved back to the car, for it did begin to seem as if the sooner they got home, the better.

"We'll have to tell Mum and Dad," said Edward. "They guess something's up, and they're sure to want to know what it is. You know Mum; she'll think some awful thing has happened, and she might as well know it's good."

Fortunately, they did not have long to wait. Their parents arrived at the same time from different directions. They were immediately pounced on and told about the lottery ticket. They found it hard to believe, but in the face of so much earnest assurance they were forced, in the end, to admit that it might be possible. As the children seemed in any case to be beside themselves with excitement, it appeared desirable to take them home. They bundled into the car, Mr. Barker started the engine, and they drove quickly out of town.

Fanny had so often stayed at home with Jack, or whoever remained behind, that it did not cross the mind of anyone that they should have had her with them.

The car had scarcely stopped when they tumbled out and raced up to the office to fetch the mailbag. Mr. Barker with due ceremony produced the key. It was opened on the veranda and the letters shaken out. A typewritten one addressed to Belinda was the last to come, and as it fell on top of the little heap, they saw printed on one corner, "State Lottery Office." With a squeak Belinda pounced on it and tore it open. No one moved as she unfolded the small piece of paper and read. She was still at the stage of mouthing all her words, and she did so now, to their fury. At last she looked up and said in a kind of whisper, "I think it says I've won fifteen pounds."

There was a silence. Then Mr. Barker, who was never silent for long, said, "Better give it to me." She handed it over, and he glanced through it. Then he looked up and nodded. "She's right," he said. Slowly and dreamily, he folded the piece of paper and handed it back.

Then Lorna looked around at Robbie, Belinda and Edward. "Let's tell Mum now," she said. "Shall we?"

At last there was nothing to stop them, so Robbie was sent off to bring the Meccano box. The others made their mother sit down, handling her with care and ceremony, as if she might come to pieces in their hands. Wondering, she sank into a chair, and Mr. Barker, looking puzzled, sat down beside her.

"What's all this about?" he asked loudly. "What's going on?"

"Wait," said Edward. "Just wait."

Mrs. Barker looked at the three faces and knew something more than ordinary was happening. Then Robbie arrived looking solemn and portentous but with a controlled excitement that threatened to break through at any moment. He laid the Meccano box at her feet and at a sign from the others opened it. Belinda dropped in the letter from the lottery office. Lorna pushed it over to her mother's feet.

"For you, Mum," she said.

"For me?" said Mrs. Barker and bent down. She looked carefully into the box. Then she looked up. "There's money in it," she said, "and a piece of paper that says I can borrow a cottage—"

"That's right," said Robbie. "Go on, Mum."

So Mrs. Barker counted the money and looked at the checks carefully, one by one. At the end, she looked at the lottery letter. Then she slowly closed the lid and looked up.

"I don't understand," she said. "There's a great deal of money here."

Smiles broke out on four faces. "Yes, isn't there?" said Edward.

Lorna came over to her mother and sat down at her feet. "We've all earned it," she said. "It's for you to go to the hospital. Because of the party, you know, when you got so tired. Take it, Mum."

Mrs. Barker looked from one to the other of her children, and the expression on her face was hard to read but, all things considered, satisfactory. "Tell me how," she said at last.

So they told her, each in turn, and as they told, things became clear to her. One by one the things that had worried her began to be sorted out and explained, and it all turned out quite obvious and nothing to be worried about at all, but on the contrary, something to be very proud of indeed.

Robbie was the last to finish, and remembering how very nearly his efforts for her had ended in disaster, she slipped an arm around his shoulder and held him tight. Then she looked up at Mr. Barker.

"Let's all have some tea," she said. "I have had a great shock, and I must be revived!" But she did not look at all as if she needed reviving.

He sprang up at once. "Yes, indeed," he said. "Yes, a splendid idea. Everybody stay here. I shall get it." He was about to disappear into the house when there was a step on the veranda, and Jack came around the corner.

"Hello," he said. "You're home earlier than I expected." He walked toward them, and as he did so, Mrs. Barker's expression changed. Her hand slowly came up to her mouth. Her eyebrows rose extremely high. Seeing this, he said, "What's the matter, Mum?"

"Fanny," she said faintly. "We've left Fanny in Bungaree."

It was Belinda's jaw that dropped the furthest. "Oh," she said. "I forgot all about her."

"Stay where you are," said Mr. Barker suddenly and loudly from the doorway. "I'll go and ring the policeman. No need to worry."

He went inside, and they heard the telephone bell ring violently. There was silence, and then they heard the murmur of his voice. There were muffled ejaculations, pauses, and quick sentences, and then there was a ring off. Mr. Barker appeared in the doorway again. His face bore an expression of utter astonishment.

"What is it, dear?" his wife asked quickly. "What's happened?"

He sat down beside her and put his hand on her knee. "Our youngest daughter," he began in a loud, clear voice, "was just about to be charged with being a neglected child. Constable North found her (as a result of a phone call) wandering from house to house in such a filthy condition that he did not recognize her. She had been soliciting money at every door and has collected quite a swag. He was delighted to have her identified, for he had not been able to get her to say anything at all. Unless we can get her to talk, it may be difficult to return the money, except to the last few houses from which her visits were reported. I told him we would go in immediately to pick her up."

For a moment no one said anything at all. Then Lorna said, "That's because she heard us last night. She's been collecting it for you, Mum."

"Oh," said her mother, "oh dear!" And then her face softened, brightened, and expanded, and she began to laugh. She laughed until her usually pale cheeks were pink and young-looking, and the tears filled her eyes. One by one they all began laughing with her—even Jack, who was usually so serious. And in the end, it was their father's jovial boom that topped them all.